TO FIND THE KILLER OF HIS FATHER AND BROTHER, BRENT HOLLISTER WOULD RISK ANYTHING—EVEN HIS LIFE!

A gun roared and Brent Hollister felt the bite of the bullet on his cheek. He jerked out his '45 and whirled, firing. Behind him another gun blazed; Brent wheeled and fired until his gun was empty.

THEN HE SAW THEM—A WHOLE BODY OF MEN ROUNDING THE CORNER, BLASTING HOT LEAD STRAIGHT AT HIM. THE ODDS WERE AGAINST HIM—THE ONLY SURE THING WAS HIS COURAGE!

RANGE JUSTICE

Paul Evan Lehman

PAPERBACK LIBRARY, Inc.
New York

PAPERBACK LIBRARY EDITION

First Printing: *September, 1964*
Second Printing: *February, 1968*

Copyright, 1950, by Star Guidance, Inc.
All Rights Reserved

All the names and characters described
in this book are fictitious, and have
no reference to any living person.

Paperback Library books are published by Paperback Library, Inc. Its trademark, consisting of the words "Paperback Library" and associated distinctive design, is registered in the United States Patent Office. Printed in the United States of America, Paperback Library, Inc., 315 Park Avenue South, New York, N.Y. 10010.

CHAPTER ONE

THOSE who knew him casually called him Tex; to the few who thought they knew him more or less intimately he had another name, Brent. They assumed that Brent was a surname but they were wrong; his name was Brent Hollister and he came from Arizona and not from Texas, but he kept the Hollister strictly to himself because the name would immediately associate him with another Hollister and that would mean sudden death.

Night had fallen and this determined young man stood in front of the closed harness shop gazing across the street towards Hannigan's store. The store was lighted and there were men inside buying tobacco and whiskey but they held no interest for Brent. His gaze was fixed on the doorway at the corner of the building which opened on the stairs leading to the hall on the second floor. Nothing could distract him at the moment.

Above that doorway a smoky kerosene torch illuminated a canvas streamer bearing the words *Sam Carter's Lyceum Players;* inside, a chubby, baldheaded man was seated behind a table and standing near him, keen-eyed and alert, was Cliff Durham, the town marshal. Money was flowing in and any amount of cash, exposed and unguarded, would have constituted a challenge to the outlaws who infested the town of Destiny.

Customers went through the doorway, paid their admissions and stamped up the stairs after receiving a cherubic smile and a hearty thank-you from Sam Carter. The smile was induced by the realization on Sam's part that this was going to be a sell-out and a sell-out meant new life for a defunct treasury, full stomachs for the troupe and, what was even more important, oat-filled bellies for the mules which drew the big wagon. It had been a long time since Sam had had a sell-out performance.

A girl came running down the stairs and the light from the

bracket lamp above Sam's head caught and held her in its yellow embrace. She was tall for a girl, but slim and graceful, with a bright face and cluster of dark curls falling over one shoulder. Brent stared interestedly; there was something clean and vibrant about her which drew him. She spoke to Sam and he nodded and she ran up the stairs, her silken-clad ankles twinkling.

Sam spoke to the marshal and Cliff Durham went outside and crossed to the store entrance. He called, "Show's ready to start, fellers!" and there was a flurry of last-minute purchases and a general exodus.

Brent took a bundle from beneath his arm and shook it out. It was a black cloth sack some six feet long and two wide. He slipped it over his head, thrusting his arms through holes cut for the purpose. It covered him from top to toe and there was a slit opposite his eyes through which he could see. He raised the bottom and drew the .44 Colt from its holster, then moved along the sidewalk fifty feet or so and crossed the dark street. He saw old man Hannigan extinguish the last lamp, come out, snap the padlock on the door and go into the hall.

Brent glided along the street, keeping close to the buildings, and mounted the store steps at an angle designed to keep him out of the range of vision of Sam and the marshal. From the hall upstairs came handclapping, whistling, the thumping of boots on the floor, and under cover of the noise Brent moved swiftly to a point just outside the doorway. The applause ceased and voices drifted down the stairs, muffled, distant, the words indistinguishable. The show had started. Brent heard Cliff Durham say to Carter, "Step outside a minute, mister."

Brent drifted silently backwards, the black hood blending with the shadows that engulfed the store entrance. Cliff came into the light and Carter came out after him. Sam hugged the metal cash box close to his paunch and there was a hint of apprehension in his eyes. He said, "I'm much obliged to you, Marshal, for your help. I'd like to give you a little—uh —token of my appreciation. Say, five dollars?"

He was looking questioningly at Cliff, the flare illuminating his fat face, but Durham did not answer. Sam raised the lid of the box, fumbled with its contents for a moment, then took out a goldpiece. He dropped it into Cliff's extended palm and Cliff said, "Keep comin'; I'll tell you when to stop."

"But, Marshal! I—"

"I said I'd tell you when to stop. Hell, if it hadn't been for me some feller'd have hung around and lifted the whole works. Now I want my reward."

"It's robbery!" moaned Sam.

"You said it," came a voice from the darkness.

Cliff wheeled, crouching like a big cat, his hand whipping to the gun at his hip. He was fast, but he didn't go through with the draw. The light fanning out from the flare showed him a hand with a leveled gun in it and that gun was pointed at his stomach. He straightened slowly, his gaze boring into the blackness. "Who are you?"

Brent said, "Get behind him, fatty, and lift that gun out of the holster. Chuck it into the street and feel him over for others. Hands up, you!"

Sam fished the Colt from its holster, flung it into the street, then patted the marshal, found the Derringer under his left arm and tossed it after the Colt. Brent said, "Line up beside him."

Carter obeyed and Brent came slowly forward, the gun still pointed at Cliff's stomach. He said, "Turn around both of you."

Carter turned instantly; Durham, reluctantly, his glinting eyes stabbing at the dark-robed figure until the last moment. Brent moved forward, halted behind Cliff, raised his Colt and struck just back of Cliff's right ear. The marshal folded up like a wet sack. Brent bent over him, took a pair of handcuffs from his belt, then said to Sam, "Down the steps and back to the stable. And I'll carry the baby; you might drop it."

The gun muzzle nudged Sam in the back and Brent heard Sam's groan as he passed back the cash box. Brent followed him into the passageway beside the store building, maintaining contact with the Colt. There was a hitching post outside the stable; he cuffed Sam to it and went away.

A hundred feet down the alley he wiggled out of the black covering, rolled it into a bundle and put it, together with the cash box, under one arm. He went through another passageway to the street and turned to his right. He had no fear of being seen, for the saloons were closed and everybody, including the honkytonk girls, had gone to the show.

He halted before a small, neat house near the end of town. There was a light in the parlor and he moved silently to a window and looked in. Luella Roselle, in robe and slippers, was curled up on a divan smoking a cigarette. She was waiting for him according to plan.

Lu Roselle, copper-haired and green-eyed, was the sister of Jack Roselle, owner of the White Palace. At least Jack said she was his sister, although the utter lack of family resemblance gave reason for doubt. Jack, slim, cold and pokerfaced, was the leader of a select group of outlaws, one of the three bands which holed up in Destiny. It was Jack who had assigned Brent the task of separating Sam Carter from his cash box.

Brent pushed the black robe into the shadows beneath the window and rounded the corner of the house and went up on the porch. He rapped sharply on the door and presently heard the shuffle of Lu's approaching feet. She said in a low, husky voice, "Who is it?" and he answered "Tex" and she slid the bolt. He stepped inside and she closed the door and locked it again. He strode through a doorway into the parlor and glanced about him appreciatively.

She spoke from behind him. "Like it?"

He turned and grinned at her and the smile lifted the left corner of his mouth slightly higher than the right and the eyebrow on that side climbed upward. It lent him an impish look and was one of the characteristics which had drawn Lu's attention. She had noticed other things: the neatness of him; the wave in his carefully brushed brown hair; the cheeks and lips which, in an age when men considered it unfashionable to allow their faces to stick up bare above their collars, were smoothly shaved; the tall, lean frame and wide shoulders with their suggestion of strength; the easy grace of his movements and the drawl which became more pronounced in moments of anger or stress.

Watching him, Lu had felt the tug of his personality as steel feels the pull of the magnet. Subtly she had tried to draw his attention and had failed; he noticed her as he noticed the other girls, as part of the furnishings. Now for the first time they had really met, and in the privacy of her own home with Jack and just about everybody else at the show.

And Brent was thinking, *This is what I've been angling for, the chance to be with her alone, to make friends, to win her confidence. She must know the man I'm looking for; if Jack has told anybody, he's told her.*

He said, "It's mighty nice. I bet it was you who picked the furniture."

The green eyes were warm, like grass under a spring sun. "Yes, I picked the stuff. Won't you sit down?"

Brent seated himself on the divan, put the cash box on the floor and deposited his hat upon it. Lu walked to a cabinet at one side of the room, opened it and took out a bottle of whiskey and two glasses. She glanced at him over her shoulder, her brows raised inquiringly. "Chaser?"

"Straight."

She crossed to the divan, gave him a glass and poured a drink for him. She sat down beside him, filled her glass and set the bottle on the floor. She said, "Luck!" and downed it like a man. He followed suit and she refilled the glasses, then settled back on the divan with a sigh of contentment. She said, "You're sort of new around here, aren't you, Tex?"

"Yes. I was lucky to be picked for tonight's job."

She laughed shortly. "One reason Jack picked you was because you're the only man in town who hasn't given me a tumble. He knew we'd be alone and he thinks you're safe. Are you?"

"Ordinarily, about as safe as a stick of dynamite with a lighted cigarette in its end. But I won't take advantage of Jack's confidence in me."

She tilted back her head and regarded him from beneath long, lowered lashes. "Entertaining a man in my own home is something of a novelty. I rather think I like it. You don't know how sick I am of the Palace and the bunch that hangs out there. They kid the other girls and dance with them and drink with them and I sit there night after night watching and smiling and pretending I like it. And I've got to go down there as soon as the show's over and do it some more."

The blood began to pound through Brent's veins. This girl, resentful, starved for affection, was giving him her confidence more easily than he had expected. He said, "That comes from having a brother ride herd on you. The other girls may have brothers too, but they're not on the spot to watch them."

She studied him, her head back-tilted. "Are you scared of Jack too?"

"No. Maybe I don't know him well enough."

"You act as though you are. Not once at the Palace have you spoken to me. I don't believe you've even looked at me."

His left eyebrow went up. "How could I help looking at you? You stand out like a rose in a patch of ragweed. I looked at you plenty when you didn't know it."

"Did you really? That calls for another drink."

"Just one more. You've got to get ready to go to the Palace and I've got to get out of here pretty soon. Cliff Durham knows the money was stolen and he may be snooping around."

They drank and Lu cuddled against him, and he was conscious of the warmth and softness of her body. She said, "If you only knew how good it feels just to be *close* to a nice man!"

He said, "It's good to be sitting here with such a lovely girl," and slipped his arm about her. She put her coppery head on his shoulder and closed her eyes. "You know," she said, "you remind me of somebody I knew. He used to work for Jack. His name was Cole, Slim Cole."

Brent's heart stopped dead, then resumed its pumping at an

increased tempo. Slim Cole was the name used by his brother when he had come to Destiny; perhaps he was about to learn that which had brought him to this outlaw town. He said carelessly, "He must have been a mighty fine man. Old or young?"

"He was young; twenty-five or six." Lu's voice was grave. "He liked me and I liked him. He used to sit at the table with me and talk. Just ordinary talk, no mush."

"Is he still around? I'd like to meet him."

"He was murdered. They found him in an alley with the back of his head shot off. When I heard about it I nearly passed out."

"Oh, that fellow! I heard some of the boys talking about it down at the Palace when I first hit town. Have they found the one who killed him?"

"No."

Brent was tingling in every nerve. If she knew who had killed his brother maybe he could get it out of her.

"Maybe Jack thought there was something more than conversation between you and this Slim Cole."

She shook her head. "We did all our talking in public and Jack often joined us. He liked Slim. It couldn't have been Jack who killed him for Jack didn't leave the Palace until it closed and then he came home with me and didn't leave the house that night."

"And our tough town marshal couldn't find out a thing?"

"No. I guess he tried hard enough but he had nothing to go on. He figured that Slim wasn't killed where he was found. A wound like that would bleed a lot and there was no blood in the alley. Slim was killed somewhere else and his body dumped there." She raised her head and flashed him a shrewd, suspicious glance. "Why are you so interested in a man you didn't even know?"

He lifted the corner of his mouth. "Just like to hear myself talk, I reckon." She seemed satisfied, but he knew he had pushed the matter as far as he dared. He withdrew his arm and said with an appearance of reluctance, "I've got to go. Cliff might take a peek through the window and see me, and I'm supposed to be in Juniper."

He got up and she extended a hand and he took it and drew her to her feet. She stood very close to him, looking up at him with veiled eyes. She said, "I've really enjoyed this, Tex. Keep your nose clean with Jack and we may have another chance to be together. Would you like that?"

"I'd like it."

"Then kiss me goodnight."

She raised her lips and he put his arms about her and kissed her. It was a long kiss and would have been longer if he hadn't pushed her gently away. He said, "Remember that stick of dynamite! Goodnight, Lu. Sorry I have to leave so soon, but we'll hope for another time."

She smiled, her green eyes warm. "You're nice, Tex. Such a change from the Palace! To think I've actually been kissed by some man other than—my brother. Now beat it; and look out for Cliff Durham."

He went through the dining room and into the kitchen, groped his way to the back door. He opened it a crack and stood looking and listening until he was satisfied that nobody was watching the place, then slipped outside, rounded the house and got the black robe and slipped into it just in case. He walked quickly to the stable and found his saddled horse in the stall where he had left it. He led the animal through a back doorway to the open range, then mounted and rode at a walk along the back of the buildings which lined the alley. He saw no movement, heard no suspicious sound.

He was nearing the faint line of road which angled to the east after leaving Destiny when it happened. Save for a soft blur of movement and the swish of the rope there was no warning, and Brent had no chance to avoid the loop which settled over his shoulders and tightened. There was a violent jerk and he was torn from the saddle and slammed down on the earth with a force that jarred the breath from his body.

CHAPTER TWO

His hand flashed for the gun at his hip even as he left the saddle, but the long robe covered it and he could not get at it. He heard a harsh voice call, *"Hold him, boy!"* and felt the rope tauten as the horse backed away. The fall had twisted the robe and he could see through the slit with only one eye, but that was enough to give him the picture. Cliff Durham had been waiting in the shadow of a barn, had seen him approach in the starlight and had roped him as he rode by. As easy as that.

His arms were pinned to his sides; he heaved himself forward in an effort to gain enough slack to permit him to lift the robe and get his gun, and he heard Cliff yell, *"Back, boy! Back!"* and once more the rope tightened as the horse moved deeper into the shadow of the barn. Brent kept thrusting himself forward because there wasn't anything else he could do and the horse kept backing away, taking up the slack as fast as he made it.

Cliff was moving along the rope at a crouching trot, his gun glinting, but the black hood was an indistinct blur against the ground and he could not be sure of his target. Brent gave another heave forward, digging in with his toes, and once more the rope went slack. Cliff yelled again, *"Back, boy!"* but there came a bump and the horse gave a squeal as it backed into the rear of the barn. It had gone as far as it could.

Cliff bent and snatched up the rope, taking up the slack himself. Brent dropped to his knees and snatched the rope himself. He got up quickly and leaned back, digging in with his heels, and Cliff was pulled violently forward. Cliff stumbled and Brent gathered in a few feet of slack before Durham regained his feet. Once more the marshal leaned back on the rope. He swore viciously. "Just for that I'll blast you clean outa that nightgown you're wearin'!" he grated. Clutching the rope with his left hand, he put all his weight upon it and the barrel of the Colt arced through the air and steadied.

Brent let go the rope and leaped, trying desperately to close with Cliff before he could get in a crippling shot, and as the rope went slack Cliff fell backwards and hit the earth so hard that the gun he had cocked exploded. Brent heard the bullet cut the air over his head, then landed sprawling atop Durham.

He found the hand with the gun in it and seized the wrist, twisting sharply. Durham squirmed, his arm giving with the twist as a boxer rolls with a punch. He clung to the gun. Brent struggled partly erect and drove a double-up knee into Cliff's groin; he heard an agonized grunt force itself from the marshal's lips. He started pounding the hand which clutched the gun against the hard ground.

Cliff struck him with his left fist. It was a hard fist and there was the power of desperation behind it. It caught Brent on the chin and felt like the kick of a mule. For a moment it stunned him and he could only cling to Cliff's gun hand. He let go Cliff's wrist with his right hand and drove his own fist hard against Cliff's chin, and Cliff's head struck the ground with a thud and for a moment he went limp. Brent gripped the gun wrist again and twisted hard and this time the Colt dropped from Cliff's fingers.

Brent sprang to his feet and kicked Durham in the head, and this time the marshal went out to stay. Brent picked up the gun and hurled it as far as he could, then pulled the robe around so that he could see through the slit and walked to his horse. He was heaving with exertion and his head still swam from Cliff's blow. He got into the saddle and sent the horse loping into the road, and after he had covered a mile he pulled to a halt and stripped the black robe from him. He rolled it into a bundle and tied it to his saddle. As yet there was no sound of pursuit, but he knew that Durham was a dogged, determined man and would stick to any trail he left.

He turned his horse away from the road and spent the next three hours confusing the trail, changing direction often, wading up or down streams, using every rocky flat and stretch of hard ground that he could find, cutting a wide half circle which eventually brought him out on the road a full ten miles from Destiny. Assured that it would take Cliff many tedious hours of daylight to untangle the snarl, he found a grassy hollow, staked out his horse and lay on a blanket to smoke and think.

The whole thing had started with the death of his father. Benjamin Hollister operated a gold exchange in an Arizona mining town. He employed one clerk, a man named Harvey Stoat. A shipment of currency had been received late one afternoon and Hollister had locked it in the vault, planning to check it after supper.

He went to the office about eight o'clock, taking Stoat with him. A witness had seen them enter the office, had heard the bolt shot, and had seen light show through a window. When at midnight Hollister had not returned to his home, his wife, becoming alarmed, notified the marshal. The marshal went to the banking rooms and found the rear door unlocked. The lamp still burned but neither of the two men were there. The vault was open and the gold gone.

They found Harvey Stoat lying unconscious in the road a few miles from town. He had been shot through the lung and was dying. At the edge of the road a bit farther on they found Hollister. He had been shot in the back and died instantly. They found a two-horse wagon, but the horses were gone. Stoat did not recover consciousness, but in his delirium kept muttering two words which sounded like *Shell* and *Destry*.

Brent and his elder brother Cole were working on different ranches and both quit their jobs to run down the killer. They gathered all the information available and reconstructed the crime.

Harvey Stoat had no family connections in town or, so far as they could learn, anywhere else, and since entrance to the banking room had not been forced they concluded that he had conspired with another to steal the currency and had unbolted the rear door before leaving with Hollister for supper. His partner had entered during their absence and had concealed himself until the vault was opened. A wagon with a team of horses had been left in the alley and Hollister had been forced to carry the currency to it and then drive some distance out of town. There he had been callously murdered. Stoat, they believed, had been shot because his partner did not trust him or did not wish to divide the loot. He had used the horses for his getaway.

They assumed that the words *Shell* and *Destry* were the murderer's name, probably Sheldon Destry, until Cole had learned that there was a town in New Mexico named Destiny. When he found out that several outlaw bands operated out of that town they had the hunch that the killer's name was Shell and that he came from Destiny. The only way to check on this was for one of them to go to Destiny; they tossed for it and Cole won the toss. He decided to take the name Slim Cole and promised to write Brent when he needed help.

Weeks went by and then Brent got a letter which had been mailed at Juniper, sixty miles from Destiny. Cole had not located anybody named Shell but believed he was on a hot trail. He had learned that the three outlaw gangs operating out of Destiny were secretly directed by one man, and he believed that this man was the man they sought. Who he was Cole did not know, but he had a crazy hunch and was going to follow it up. He asked Brent to meet him in Juniper two weeks later.

Brent had gone to Juniper, but Cole had not appeared. At the end of a week he set out for Destiny. There he had heard two men talking about the mysterious murder of Slim Cole. They were wondering about it because Slim had had no enemies that they knew of and his money had not been taken.

Brent had not dared to question, but the cruel murder of his brother convinced him that the murderer of his father had somehow learned Cole's identity and had promptly removed him. Now it was up to Brent to find that man.

He remained in Destiny awaiting the chance to join one of the outlaw bands. One bunch, under Jack Roselle, staged train holdups; a second, led by Shotgun Clem Cuthbert, did highway jobs; the third, under the direction of Biff Williams, concerned themselves with banks. No two gangs struck at the same time or in the same locality. Brent knew now why Cole had concluded that the three outfits were secretly directed by one man.

Jack Roselle was the one Brent had picked to concentrate on first, and from the beginning he had realized that the key to Jack's secrets lay in Luella. To approach her in the obvious way would only earn Jack's suspicion, so he had ignored her, awaiting the proper opportunity. That opportunity had come when Jack ordered him to hold up Sam Carter. He had considered the assignment as a test of his ability and had determined not to fall down on the job no matter how distasteful it might be. And now he had met Lu and had learned the details about Cole's death. He had also learned that Jack had an alibi for the night Cole was killed. And he had learned that Cole had been murdered elsewhere and his body carried to the alley and dumped there.

Find the man who had done that and he was convinced he would find the murderer of their father. Finding that man was the task to which he had dedicated himself regardless of the depths of outlawry in which he might be plunged. He had always been law-abiding, but now he would break every law in the book, if it were necessary, to get his hands on that man.

Knowledge that Lu had noticed the resemblance between himself and Cole disturbed him, and he wondered if others would notice it too. He decided this was unlikely; the two brothers were entirely different in build and mannerisms, and Lu had noticed a faint, intangible family resemblance only because she had been unusually interested in both of them.

The lack of any disturbance following the holdup puzzled him. He could understand Cliff Durham's silence; Cliff was not a man to squeal when he was hurt but he could be counted on to stalk his man like he would a deer and dispose of him promptly when he caught up with him. But Sam Carter should have raised an outcry to high heaven, and so far as Brent knew he had not done so.

The explanation came quickly. A distant sound reached Brent and he sat up and ground out his cigarette. Presently he was able to distinguish the creak of wheels, the rattle of traces, the patter of hoofs. He got up and moved toward the road, dodging among the trees. A sliver of moon had appeared and bathed the road with its soft radiance and into this glow came a covered wagon drawn by six mules. A chubby man in a beaver hat sat on the seat beside the driver.

Brent grinned and turned back towards his camp. The Lyceum Players, their treasury depleted, had left Destiny without the formality of paying their bills. Now he understood why Sam Carter had not given the alarm; if the hotel proprietor and the owners of the livery corral and the hall knew that the company was without funds, their equipment would be seized and sold to satisfy their creditors and Sam Carter's Lyceum Players would find themselves stranded in what to them would be the middle of nowhere. Sam had used his head.

Cliff Durham would be sent after them, of course, but Brent doubted that Cliff would try to find them. If they got away, nobody would learn of the holdup and Cliff's prestige as a courageous officer of the law and a gunman without peer would not suffer. No, Cliff would not bring them back; but he would stick to the trail of the black hooded bandit like grim death, and if he ever caught up with him would settle the debt with lead.

Brent's mouth lifted in a grin as he rolled in his blankets, and the grin remained after he had fallen asleep. His dreams were pleasant ones, but they were not about a copper-haired, green-eyed beauty named Lu Roselle. He was visioning a tall, slim, dark-haired girl running lightly down the steps and speaking to Sam Carter. He dreamed he was going to meet her, and later he thought how ridiculous this was because even then that girl was jolting along the road to Juniper and out of his life.

CHAPTER THREE

JUDITH CLANE opened her eyes, blinked at the sunlight which filtered through the window, then closed them again with a sigh of contentment. No need to get up until noon. The treasury of Sam Carter's Lyceum Players had been replenished; there was money to pay their hotel bills, money to buy grain for the mules. There might be enough left to pay the troupe something on account of back salaries. Judy cuddled up and drifted off to sleep again.

She was awakened by the rattling of her door and a harsh voice shouting, "Open up in there! Open up, I say!"

Judy got up and reached for her robe, indignation stirring her. The rattling was succeeded by a thumping on the door and she called, "All right, all right! Keep your shirt on."

She pushed her feet into bedroom slippers and crossed to the door. She unlocked it and two men entered. One she recognized as the hotel clerk, the other she had not seen before. She said angrily, "What's the idea? This is my room and I didn't invite you in."

"You're wrong," said the strange man nastily. "I own the hotel and it's *my* room. I rent it to you with your meals for two dollars a day. You can pay me for it right now." He was small and fat and well manicured, but anger had robbed him of any chivalry he might have possessed.

Judy said stiffly, "Mr. Carter will pay you. He's manager of the company and handles all the finances."

"Mr. Carter," said the fat man viciously, "pulled out last night, wagon, mules and everything else but you."

"Oh, no!" said Judy.

"Oh, yes!" said the fat man.

"But he couldn't have!" Apprehension seized her with a chill hand. "He had the money to pay. The house was sold out last night."

"And I was sold out, too. But as soon as I can round up Cliff Durham he'll go after them and fetch them back. In the meantime you dig up the two dollars you owe for your room and board and if you want to stay here you'll cough up two dollars every day and strictly in advance."

Judy backed away and sat heavily on the bed. She felt sick and very much alone. "But I haven't two dollars," she said. "I haven't even a dollar. Sam hadn't paid us for weeks."

The fat man gave her a mean look, then turned to the clerk. "All right, George; gather up her stuff."

The clerk moved towards her valise which stood opened on a chair and Judy leaped to forestall him. The fat man interposed an arm and sent her reeling back to the bed. "Oh, no you don't!"

"But they're my clothes, all I own! You can't take them!"

The clerk put the lid on the valise and strapped it shut. Judy ran around the bed and grabbed up the clothes she had worn the night before. Her gilt slippers and silk hose were under the bed and she snatched them up too. She clutched them to her and glared at them over the bed. The clerk was taking her gowns and hats and shoes out of the clothes closet. She cried,

"Any one of those dresses will pay your bill! You can't take them all!"

"Is that so?" sneered the fat man. "Just watch and see if we can't. And you have just ten minutes to get out of this room. If you're not out by then we'll put you out."

He motioned to the clerk and the man went out carrying her valise, her gowns and hats and shoes draped over his person. The fat man gave her a jerky nod to lend emphasis to the ultimatum and followed. He took the door key with him.

Judy stared after them for a moment, then sat down on the bed, the clothing still hugged to her. The company had gone. They had gone and left her. What would she do? Where could she go? She had just sixteen cents to her name. The answer was obvious; she must get a job of some kind and she must get it at once. She had eaten no breakfast and they would give her no dinner. And tonight there would be no place to sleep.

She set about dressing. She had only the outfit she had worn the night before, a yellow evening gown with plenty of ruffles on the bottom and practically nothing at the top. She brushed out her dusky hair and twisted the curls with her fingers. She rolled the bedroom slippers in the robe and tucked the bundle under her arm. She did it all mechanically, a cold hand gripping her heart. The fat man and the clerk came upstairs and looked into the room. Her ten minutes were up. Judy walked past them with her chin in the air and descended the stairs to the lobby.

Men were lounging there and they stared at her as she walked quickly to the door and out to the street. Her eyes were bright and there were two spots of color in her cheeks. She turned right, walking rapidly. She wanted to get away from there.

The yellow gown and bare shoulders drew immediate attention. Men along the street whistled and called after her. She hurried on, glancing to right and left in search of some place that she could enter, some shop that offered a prospect of a job. She passed a harness and saddle shop, a barber shop, three saloons. At the end of the street she crossed to the other side and turned back. More saloons. A grain and feed store. No dress shop, no millinery store. A shack with the words *Gold Exchange* painted on the window. Another saloon.

A man stepped through the swinging doors and stood looking at her. He was big and rough and wore a heavy stubble of red whiskers. His eyes were reddish in color, like those of a bull. She halted, turned and looked about her in desperation. There were three men coming along the street behind her and she knew they were following her. The red-whiskered man said, "Come along, honey, and I'll buy you a drink."

She ran to the doorway of the shack with *Gold Exchange* on its window and backed into it. She couldn't speak; she just stared at him dumbly. He came slowly towards her, one big hand outthrust like a man about to capture a cornered bird. He was grinning and she saw his teeth were broken and uneven and badly stained with tobacco. He said, "Aw, come on; I ain't gonna hurt you."

The three who had been following her stopped; the man turned to them and said, "I'm roundin' up this maverick. Beat it."

One of them said, "Sure, Shotgun," and they went on their way.

"I'm Shotgun Clem Cuthbert," said the man as though that fixed everything. "You come along and we'll have some fun."

She said, "No—please!"

The door behind her opened and Judy spun about to face this new menace. She saw a big, bluff man with a neatly trimmed beard and moustache and a pair of twinkling blue eyes. His hair was carefully brushed and he wore a suit of black broadcloth. He gave her a quick, surprised glance, then spoke to Cuthbert over his shoulder. "What's the trouble, Shotgun?" The voice was mild.

"No trouble at all. I jest stopped this dolly and offered to buy her a drink. She's just playin' hard to get. Hell, ain't nobody but a honkytonk gal goes around dressed thataway."

Judy turned to the big man and tried to speak calmly. "Listen, mister. I'm one of Sam Carter's players. The little weasel pulled out last night and left me stranded. I haven't any money and the hotel people took all my clothes but these. I've got to find a job. I just have to!"

"Sure, sure." He smiled down on her and patted her reassuringly on the shoulder. He said to Cuthbert in the same mild voice, "You see how it is, Shotgun. You got this young lady wrong. She's down on her luck and I know you wouldn't take advantage of her misfortune, would you?"

Cuthbert shuffled his feet uncomfortably. "Well—no. No, Uncle Jim, I sure wouldn't be that lowdown. I just thought—" He waved his hand in a vague, wondering gesture, then said abruptly, "Hell!" and slouched away.

The man said, "Come into the office and tell me about it, huh?"

Warmth came back into Judy's body and she looked gratefully at him. "Thanks a lot, mister—"

19

"Ferguson. James Ferguson. But everybody around here calls me Uncle Jim."

He led the way inside and waved her into a chair. Judy sank into the chair and he lowered himself into one before a desk and smiled at her. "Now tell me all about it."

She told him swiftly. "I don't know why Sam ducked out. He had the money to pay. Last night was a sell-out."

He nodded. "I'm wondering how you happened to be left behind."

She told him frankly; he had befriended her and was entitled to her full confidence. "It wasn't an accident. Lately, since we've been having hard luck, the company has been doubling up in hotel rooms to save expense. Sam was angry at me because—because I wouldn't share his room with him."

"I see. Did you share your room with anybody else?"

"No. I was an odd girl; I always took a single room. Towards the end I paid for it myself to keep Sam from grumbling. That's why I'm broke now. Mr. Ferguson, I've got to find something to do; I've just got to get a job."

"Finding a job in a town like this, Miss—I don't believe you've told me your name."

"I'm Judith Clane." She smiled faintly. "My friends call me Judy."

"Then I'll call you Judy too." He swung about in the chair and stared for some moments at the wall. At last he turned back to her. "You're a professional entertainer; you might get something to do in that line." He got up briskly and took a hat from a clothes tree. "Suppose you sit right here while I go out and scout around a bit, huh?"

"Oh, would you?"

"Glad to. I won't be long. Had your dinner yet?"

"No, sir, but I'm really not hungry."

He nodded and went out and Judy drew a sigh of relief and relaxed in the chair. He was a swell egg; anybody that folks called Uncle Jim would be. Gosh, she was lucky to find a friend like him in this tough town!

He was back within ten minutes carrying a tray of steaming food. He set it on the desk and said, "Pull up your chair and wrap yourself around this."

"Really, Uncle Jim, I shouldn't let you—"

He cut her short with a wave of his big hand. "You can pay me back when you get the job." He left quickly and Judy was just finishing the dinner when he came back. He appeared pleased. He said, "Well, I've got a job for you. You're to sing a few songs at Jack Roselle's White Palace and work with the other girls?"

She said doubtfully, "Work with—the other girls?"

"Play up to the customers a little, get them to gamble and buy drinks. You get a commission on what they spend."

Her voice was steady. "Is that all?"

"Sure. Oh, men'll say things and do things, especially when they're drinking, but if you show them you're on the square they won't bother you. Jack's sister sort of looks out for the girls and she's as straight as a string." He regarded her steadily for a moment then asked, "Would you rather that I lend you enough money to rejoin the company?"

She shook her head. "Sam doesn't want me and I have no home to go to. My parents are dead; I have—nobody. I took a job with the show because I knew there were wonderful opportunities in the West for people who aren't afraid. I even thought—" she glanced shyly at him—"that out here I might meet the—the right man." She laughed embarrassedly. "Silly, isn't it? But girls do dream. Even showgirls."

"Then you haven't been a showgirl long?"

"This is my first trip on the road. It's fascinating work and—" she regarded him steadily—"I've kept to the straight and narrow path, Uncle Jim." She gave him a faint smile. "Perhaps I was thinking of that man I might meet." She didn't know why she was confiding in him like this except that he was so understanding. It was like talking to one's father.

He said, "I see. Well, do you want that job?"

"Of course I do."

"Good girl! Come along and I'll introduce you to your boss."

They walked along the street together. Her hand was in the crook of his arm and the big solid frame beside her reassured her and gave her courage.

They went through the swinging half-doors of the White Palace. A man was leaning against the bar smoking a thin cigar. He was of average height but rather slight of build, dark-haired and neat, with a small waxed moustache and side burns. He had gray eyes that were as cold as frozen agates.

Ferguson said, "This is Judy Clane, Jack. Judy, Mr. Roselle."

Jack said without any expression, "The girls have rooms upstairs; come on up and I'll show you where to bunk."

They went through a doorway and up a flight of stairs, then along a corridor with doors on both sides. Jack opened one of these and went in and Judy and Ferguson followed him. It was a small, unpapered room with one window. There was a chest of drawers, washstand, two chairs and a double bed. A girl in a soiled kimona was stretched out on the bed reading a paper-backed novel. Her yellow hair streamed over the pillow. Jack said, "Brought you a roommate, Lil. Judy Clane."

The girl said, "Hi-yuh, kid! Hi-yuh, Uncle Jim!" She swung her legs off the bed and sat up. "Say! I seen you at the show last night, didn't I? You're damned right I did! Welcome to the brothel!"

"Look after her, Lil," said Jack. "Come along, Uncle Jim."

Judy turned to Ferguson and put out her hand. "Thanks awfully, Uncle Jim!"

The blue eyes twinkled. "Don't mention it, Judy. You'll be seeing me again; I drop in every once in a while." He gave her hand a reassuring pressure and went out after Jack, closing the door.

"Sit down, kid," invited Lil. "I got a bottle hid away; we'll have a snort and then you can tell me all about it."

CHAPTER FOUR

SMALL as the job had been, Jack Roselle had arranged an alibi for Brent. On the morning the holdup, and in the presence of the marshal, Jack had ordered Brent to Juniper on some trumped-up errand, and Brent, after beefing a bit over having to miss the show, had started out. He had not gone to Juniper, of course, but had camped a few miles from town and remained there until dark. Then he had stolen into town, put his horse in Jack's stable and pulled the holdup. When he escaped from Cliff he made camp knowing that he would have to remain away from Destiny until the following evening, when he would ride into town on a wet horse, his alibi riding with him.

He timed his arrival to coincide with the supper hour, went into the Palace for a drink and saw Jack standing in his accustomed place at the end of the bar. It was too early for business and the place was nearly empty. He went over to where Jack stood and asked in a low voice, "Get it?"

"Yes. Trouble?"

"None to speak of."

"Cliff hasn't been seen since last night. I wondered."

He did not ask for details and Brent volunteered none. "I'll have a quick one and then wrap myself around some grub."

He poured himself a drink from the bottle Jack pushed towards him, said, "Be seeing you," and went out. Near the end of town was a Chinese restaurant and he entered it. A couple of girls sat at a table in the back of the gloomy room and one of them waved a plump hand and called, "Hi-yuh, Tex!" It was Lil, the vivid blonde with the big bosom and wide smile. He raised a hand in salute and then recognized the other girl. His eyes widened in surprise; the yellow gown, the dark curls—it was the girl he had seen descending the stairs to speak to Sam Carter, the girl he had dreamed he was going to meet.

She glanced up from her plate and he raised his hat. She gave him a fleeting, timid smile and lowered her eyes again. Brent turned and went to the counter; he was so dazed that the waiter had to ask twice for his order.

"Huh? Oh! Tenderloin steak, a hatful of hashed browns, stewed tomatoes and half an apple pie. That'll take the edge off."

The waiter shuffled off. Brent glanced covertly at the girls' table; Lil was talking with her mouth full, the dark-haired girl ate slowly, her gaze lowered. What in hell was she doing in Destiny? She should be with Carter's outfit somewhere in the vicinity of Juniper.

He ate mechanically. He heard the scrape of their chairs when they got up, the click of high heels as they came along the row of counter stools. Lil stopped behind him, put an arm about his shoulder and leaned over to whisper, "How do you like her? Ain't she a honey?"

"She sure is. Where'd you find her?"

"Sam Carter pulled out last night and left her." She turned, pulling Brent around with her. "Hey, kid! Come over here and shake hands with a good guy. This is Tex, Judy; Tex, meet up with Judy Clane."

Brent got to his feet and took off his hat. He didn't know why he did it, it was an entirely unconscious gesture. The girl came towards him, a faint smile on her lips. She held out her hand and he took it. She was looking at him directly now and he saw that her lashes were long and dark and the eyes a rich, warm brown. She said, "I'm glad to know you, Tex."

"Not half as glad as I am to know you, Judy."

Lil said, "We gotta rustle our hocks; come on, kid. Hey, Tex! For Pete's sake, let her go!"

Brent looked down, saw that he was still holding Judy's hand and relinquished it. She gave him a quick smile and went out with Lil. He went back to the counter and sat down on the wrong stool. He rectified the mistake, feeling foolish, and finished his supper. He strolled around town and finally turned into the Palace. The place was filling up and most of the gambling layouts were running; the girls had come downstairs and were moving about, soliciting drinks.

Judy was doing her best, calling upon her showgirl experience to help. There were three men at the bar with her and she was laughing and drinking with them and occasionally one of them would give her an affectionate hug. Brent went to the bar and called for a drink.

Shotgun Clem Cuthbert came in and bellied the bar beside him. Cuthbert led the bunch that specialized in highway robbery. He was big and tough and his clothes always looked as though he had just picked himself up after a rough-and-tumble fight. His right shoulder had been injured by a bullet and he was unable to raise a rifle to his shoulder, so he had taken to using a shot gun loaded with buckshot which he fired from the waist. He watched Judy in the backbar mirror for a while, then slouched along the counter to join the group which surrounded her.

One of these was Biff Williams, leader of the bank gang. There was no love lost among the three gangs and Brent saw that Williams resented Shotgun's horning in. Biff was even bigger than Cuthbert, with heavy black brows, a fierce black moustache and very penetrating black eyes; but his clothing was clean and well fitting and his boots always shone. He was a good shot but preferred to use his hands. He could hit like a sledgehammer and had the strength to strangle a bull.

Uncle Jim Ferguson stepped into the place Shotgun had vacated and said, "How are you, Tex?" He too was watching the group in the mirror. Tex said he was fine and they had a drink. "The little lady is going to have trouble on her hands," said Ferguson. "I'm afraid she's overdoing it a little. Nice kid. Have you met her yet?"

"Lil introduced me at the restaurant."

"She was a mighty scared girl today." He told Brent of her encounter with Shotgun. "I got her this job and I sort of feel responsible for her. I guess I'd better go down there and break it up."

He joined the group and presently Brent heard his hearty voice boom out and caught Judy's nervous laugh as she walked with him to a table. They sat down and Ferguson ordered beer. Nobody else, thought Brent, could have taken her from the two outlaw leaders without a fight, but Uncle Jim was everybody's friend. He bought and sold gold and spent a lot of time traveling from one mining camp to another.

"Howdy, Tex; how's tricks?"

A disreputable old man had slipped up to the bar. His Levi's were clean but covered with patches of many sizes and colors; his cheap cotton shirt had worn through at the elbows and his boots were run down at the heels and broken out at the toes. His hat was a misshapen thing with a brim that drooped wearily as though yearning for the peace of the village dump.

He was a little, wizened man, an outlaw considered now too old for active service. His dried-apricot face was covered with a stubble of gray, he wore a scraggly, dejected moustache and had cut his hair with a pair of sheep shears. The most remarkable thing about him were his eyes; they were a bright blue but so crossed that no one could be certain just where he was looking. His name was Bub Whittaker but they called him the Cockeyed Kid.

Brent grinned down at him. The old man was cheerful and friendly and Brent liked him. He said, "Belly up, Bub, and we'll toss off a few."

"Thank-ee, Tex, we'll shore do that. And some day I'm gonna buy you a drink outa the income on my debts."

They had a drink, then Brent said, "Let's buy a bottle and take it over to a table. You can tell me about the good old days when men were men and women were glad of it."

They took the bottle to a table and sat down and the Cockeyed Kid started his tale. It was a wild one of misspent youth and the owlhoot trail and Brent listened without really hearing what the old fellow said. He was watching the leaders of the three gangs, Jack Roselle, Biff Williams and Shotgun Cuthbert. Logic said that one of these three was the man who planned the jobs and assigned them, and he hoped to determine which he was by his actions. But the only time Biff and Clem were together was when they were pestering Judy and neither of them went near Jack Roselle.

The whiskey level in the bottle lowered steadily, but it was not Brent who drank, and presently he heard a snore and turned his head. The Cockeyed Kid had tilted his chair against the wall, pulled his battered Stetson over his crossed eyes and was asleep.

Time drifted by. Ferguson was finally forced to relinquish Judy to the mercies of Biff and Shotgun. Lu Roselle was at her accustomed place at a table; she did not glance towards Brent and he did not look at her. Jack Roselle finally spoke to a bartender and the man pushed to the rear of the room and mounted the platform. He yelled for quiet and said, "Fellers, we got a little lady with us tonight who seems to be mighty popular. Reckon most of you heard her at the show last night. She's gonna sing some songs for us."

He jumped from the platform and seated himself at the piano, and Judy was lifted to the stage by Biff and Clem. She was laughing, but Brent thought he could read fright in her eyes. She sang some of the songs she had sung the night before and the men yelled their approval. When she finally left the stage she was surrounded and carried to the bar. One drink followed another in quick succession and Brent found himself frowning. He wondered just how much she could take, then swore under his breath and asked himself what the hell he cared.

The end came suddenly. Judy, with Biff and Shotgun sticking close to her, walked unsteadily to a table. Her cheeks were flushed and the brown eyes were glazed. She almost fell into a chair and went limp on the table, out cold.

Lu Roselle said sharply, "Take care of her, Lil."

Lil went to the table, shook Judy and said, "Snap out of it, kid! Come on; you're goin' to bed. You hear me? Snap out of it." There was no response; Judy's reactions were those of a rag doll. Lil glanced about helplessly. "One of you birds give me a hand; I can't lug her upstairs all by myself."

Biff Williams said, "I'll carry her up and put her to bed."

"You will like hell!" shouted Cuthbert. "I'll take care of her."

They argued the matter, each claiming prior rights, until Jack Roselle came from the bar and interrupted them. "Cut it out, boys. Settle it some way, but get her out of here."

The two men exchanged glares for a moment longer, then Biff said, "If you could play poker, I'd play you a hand of showdown, Clem."

"I'll take you on and six others like you," said Shotgun. "Get a deck."

Brent got up and walked towards the table. He didn't know why; something stronger than his will propelled him. Williams got a deck from the faro dealer and started riffling the cards. Brent said, "Deal me in."

They gave him a stare and Biff said, "This ain't your party, Tex."

"Three'll make it more interesting. Deal me in."

"This is private between me and Biff," growled Shotgun.

Brent drawled, "Biff represents the bank crowd, you the highway bunch. Deal me in for the train crowd."

Jack Roselle said shortly, "Let him in on it."

They did not sit down. Shotgun took the cards from Biff. "You ain't dealin' and I ain't dealin' and Tex ain't dealin'." He looked slowly about him and his gaze fell on the sleeping Whittaker. He yelled, "Hey, Cockeye!"

Bub's head came up with a jerk and he blinked at the light. "Huh?"

"Come over here and deal out a hand."

Bub got up slowly, still blinking, and came over to the table. Williams explained. "You'll deal a hand of showdown to Clem and Tex and me. The winner puts the girl to bed." He nodded towards the sleeping Judy.

The Cockeyed Kid took the deck and shuffled clumsily. He spilled some cards and said apologetically, "Sorta outa practice, boys. Mebbe I'm gittin' old." He slapped the deck in front of Tex and said, "Cut."

There was a tiny break near the middle and a hunch told Brent to cut at that point. Bub picked up the deck. "Face up?" he asked.

"Face up," approved Biff. "Everybody sees what we're gittin'."

Men were whispering, making side bets. Even the girls had gathered about the table to watch. Shotgun's reddish eyes were on Judy, resting avidly on the bare shoulders with the dark hair tumbling over them.

The first card dealt to Williams was a jack, Cuthbert got a six, Brent a nine. Biff's second card was another jack and Brent saw a flicker of satisfaction cross his face. Shotgun drew a deuce and cursed. Brent's card was a king. Whittaker gave Williams a five and Shotgun whooped when he got another six. Brent drew a three. Williams now had a pair of jacks, Cuthbert a pair of sixes. Brent king high.

Slowly Bub dealt the fourth card to Williams. It was a ten. Shotgun got a seven, Brent a second nine. The men were commenting in low voices; these hands were surprizingly high.

The last card to Williams was an ace. Cuthbert yelled, "Hit me!" and yelled louder when a second six fell. Two pairs. Williams swore and brushed his hand to the floor. Somebody said, "A buck'll get you ten that Tex don't beat those two pairs."

Lil shouted, "I'll take that, sucker!"

The Cockeyed Kid dealt Brent his last card. It was a third nine.

There was an instant of dead silence, then bedlam. Lil yelled. "Gimme that sawbuck, sucker!" and tucked the bill under a garter. She said to Lu Roselle, "That Judy kid's playin' in luck, havin' Tex put her to bed, ain't she?"

Lu said, "Yeah," and rubbed her cigarette savagely on a tray.

Brent got his right arm beneath Judy's knees and his left below her shoulders. He raised her from the chair and her dark head lolled against his chest. Jack Roselle opened the door in the side of the room and Brent started up the stairs with his burden. The jolting disturbed Judy; she twisted in his arms and muttered quickly, "Wha's—goin'—on?"

He kissed the top of her head. "Papa's putting baby to bed."

"Don' wanna—go to bed."

A lamp in a wall bracket burned in the upstairs hall and the door to Lil's room stood open. Brent put Judy on the bed, closed the door, then struck a match and lighted the lamp on the washstand. He took off his coat and tossed it on the bed. Judy was a showgirl, she had probably been around. He went over and stood looking down at her, and suddenly a wave of tenderness swept over him. He said, "Judy!"

She said, "What?" and sat up. Her eyes were dazed but the dullness had left them. She looked quickly about her, realized where she was and got up. Her knees were so weak that she sat down on the bed again. She stared at him with frightened eyes, then covered her face with her hands and began to cry.

Brent said, "We played a hand of showdown for the fun of putting you to bed. Shotgun Cuthbert, Biff Williams and I. I won, but I reckon you're able to get into bed without help. From now on watch your drinking. The next time one of the others might win."

The shoulders ceased their convulsive heaving and she raised her eyes to look at him. What she saw on his face pushed away the terror and brought wonder and gratitude into them. She said, "Oh, Tex!" and her voice broke.

She stood up and they were but six inches apart. Impulsively she put her arms about his neck and raised her lips. "You deserve something for winning and I want to give you—what I can."

He drew her close and kissed her. Her lips were soft and sweet like those of a lovely child. She whispered, "As a honky-tonk girl I'm a terrible disappointment, aren't I?"

He said deliberately, "I think you're the most wonderful kid in the world. Now get in bed and go to sleep."

He went out and closed the door, her soft, "Goodnight, Tex!" following him. He felt a bit dazed himself.

CHAPTER FIVE

BRENT went down the stairs, opened the door and entered the barroom. The excitement aroused over the poker hand had not abated; winners of bets were buying drinks and still marveling at the strength of the hands. His entrance silenced them. Biff Williams said dryly, "Fast work, Tex."

Tex leaned against the closed door. He raised an eyebrow and asked, "What's the matter? I was supposed to put her to bed. She's in bed."

"Musta been a tough job," said Biff. "You lost your coat doin' it."

Brent realized then that he had forgotten his coat; it was still on Judy's bed. He said, "I never wear a coat on Wednesday nights."

Shotgun Cuthbert came slouching around the end of the bar, a wolfish grin showing his stained teeth. "You're apt to ketch cold, sonny boy; I'll run upstairs and get it for you."

Brent did not budge from the door. "Don't bother. I'll get it when I want it."

Reddish eyes met cold blue ones in a long stare, then Shotgun shrugged and turned away, passing it off as a joke. "If you ketch lung fever, don't blame me," he said over his shoulder, and returned to the bar.

Lil came up to Brent and peered intently into his face. "I haven't seen one for so long I didn't recognize it," she said softly.

"Recognize what?"

"A gentleman. Come up to the bar, Tex; I'm buyin' you a drink. Come on, I mean it. Didn't I take Frisco Pete for ten bucks on that hand of yours?"

They went to the bar and Lil said to the bartender, "Gimme three fingers of rye, Harry, and none of that sheep dip in the bar bottle. Call your shot, Tex."

They had their drink and Brent said, "Thanks, Lil," and sauntered away. He was still watching Williams and Cuthbert and Roselle. Biff and Shotgun were at opposite ends of the bar Jack was talking with Uncle Jim Ferguson. As Brent passed Lu Roselle's table she called softly, "Tex!"

He turned to stare at her. "You talking to me?"

"Yes. Sit down." His eyebrow went up and she said impatiently. "I want to ask you about the girl."

He seated himself reluctantly. He didn't like this but even a glance towards Jack Roselle would be a giveaway. He pushed back his hat and looked at her coldly. "What do you want to know?"

She signaled the bartender with two fingers. "This is on the house," she told Brent. "Business." She had raised her voice. "How is she?"

"Asleep," he answered in the same tone.

"The little fool should know better. From here on she drinks tea."

The bartender brought their drinks; they raised the glasses and drank. Lu said without moving her lips and in a low voice, "Have a nice time?"

He didn't answer. He got up, said politely, "Thanks for the drink, Lu. I think she'll be all right in the morning." He walked away, leaving her staring after him. Confound the girl, where were her senses? Jack never missed a thing and now that he'd established contact Brent was more anxious than ever to preserve the appearance of utter indifference on the part of both of them.

He sat down in a chair and tilted back against the wall, still watching. If, for instance, one of the three engaged another in conversation and immediately afterwards that other led his gang on a raid, Brent could assume that the word had been passed and that the one who passed it was the one who did the planning.

Ferguson looked around, spotted Brent and came over to sit in the chair beside him. "Judy all right?" he asked.

"She was when I left her."

"Did you have—any trouble?"

"No. She snapped out of it by the time I got her upstairs. I left her there."

"I'm glad to hear that, Tex. I feel sorry for the girl. And responsible, in a way. I'm going on a buying trip tomorrow; I wish you'd sort of keep an eye on her for me while I'm gone, will you?"

Brent said gruffly, "I can't be riding herd on every girl that comes to the Palace. She knows by now what she's up against."

"I know, but do the best you can. You're different from the rest of them, Tex. I've noticed it from the first. You're edu-

30

cated, you have manners, you're clean. There's not another man in Destiny I'd ask to do this." He got up. "I'm going to turn in; have to get an early start. See you when I get back." He nodded and went out.

Brent sighed. Why in hell did he have to get mixed up in this girl's affairs? Because he had got Judy the job, Uncle Jim was playing guardian, and now he had wished the job on Brent.

He got up and went over to the bar. He ordered a drink and was toying with it when he happened to glance towards the doorway. Coming along the aisle between game layouts and bar was Cliff Durham and his intent gaze was fixed on Brent. He was a formidable appearing man, short and stocky and muscular, with yellow hair and moustache and light blue eyes. He was sure death with a six-gun and while he knew plenty of four-letter words, fear was not one of them. The area about his right temple where Brent's boot had struck him was swollen and blue.

He came up to where Brent was standing and halted and his eyes did their best to drill a hole in Brent's composure. Brent said, "You run into a door?"

"Hoss kicked me." He ordered a drink and when it had been poured said, "When did you get back to town?"

"Somewhere around supper time. They tell me you've been missing all day; did you fetch Carter's outfit back?"

"Whadda you mean, fetch 'em back?"

"They pulled out last night without paying their bills."

"No, I wasn't chasin' Carter." His head came around and the pale blue eyes held Brent. "Who did you see in Juniper?"

The answer came from behind Brent and it came in Jack Roselle's toneless voice. "Tex went there for me, Cliff, and unless you've got a good reason for asking he's not going to tell you who he saw."

"All right, skip it. Where's your hoss?"

"Down at the livery corral."

"Got any objections to my lookin' him over?"

"Nope. But he's not for sale."

Cliff turned away and Jack said, "Anything on that horse?"

"Nothing that Cliff's looking for."

He had been watching Biff and Shotgun and his attention had been distracted by Cliff; now he looked again to check their positions he saw that Shotgun was no longer there. He glanced quickly towards the doorway; Shotgun was just passing through the exit to the street. Well, that meant one less to watch.

It was clear enough that Cliff suspected him and wanted to check his horse and rig. There was nothing to betray him; he had hidden the black robe in a tree outside Destiny where it would be accessible if he needed it again; his horse's shoes were evenly worn, with no broken calks. Cliff would find nothing at all, but he would keep on trying.

Trouble, thought Brent, was sure enough piling up. Cliff was on his trail, Lu Roselle had lost her caution, Biff Williams and Shotgun Cuthbert were sore at him and Ferguson had wished the job of riding herd on Judy Clane on him. The thought of her brought a sudden warm tingling; he could picture her sleeping, the long lashes curled over her cheeks, the dusky hair tumbled about the pillow. Well, he had done his share thus far; she was safe—

A sudden thought jarred him. She would never be safe while Shotgun was around. Where had the fellow gone? He rarely went home until the Palace closed. There was a rear entrance to the stairs which led to the rooms of the girls, an entrance they used when they did not want to pass through the saloon. Brent turned abruptly, passed Jack Roselle at the end of the bar and reached for the knob of the door in the side wall. He caught Jack's cold gaze on him and said, "Reckon I'll get my coat before I forget it."

He opened the door quietly, stepped through it and closed it after him. The lamp in the corridor above shed a pale glow over the landing that made the bottom of the stairs a well of darkness in comparison. A man was at the top of the stairs, mounting the step carefully and softly. Clem Cuthbert. His back was turned and he had not heard the door open and close.

Brent ducked low and tilted his face downward just in time. Shotgun halted on the landing and turned to look down the steps into the blackness, then tip-toed along the hall and out of Brent's sight.

Brent mounted the stairs at a crouching, noiseless run. His jaws were tight and his eyes glinted with anger. Again he was moved by an impulse that he did not have time to analyze. He reached the top of the stairs. Shotgun was not in sight but the door to Lil's room now stood open.

He heard Judy's startled scream, then her cry. *"Tex!"*

Her desperate appeal did something to him. He forgot utterly the caution to which he had schooled himself, knew only a red rage that made him want to strike and kill. He ran down the hall without bothering to silence his footsteps and swung into the doorway. Cuthbert was seated on the edge of the bed wrestling with a panic-stricken Judy. He was crushing her to him, bending avidly over her, reaching for her lips with his. Brent's fingers dug savagely into hat and red hair and jerked.

Shotgun's head snapped back and he let out a howl. He dropped Judy and the fierce tug brought him to his feet. He leaped backwards and his hat came away in Brent's hands. Shotgun stabbed for the gun at his hip and Brent flung the hat into his face and leaped forward. He hit Shotgun on the chin with a blow whose impact sent pain shooting up his arm.

He bored in recklessly, disregarding the menace of the gun. He did not think to draw his own .44; he wanted to hit, to maim. Shotgun staggered back under the rain of blows, crashed into the washstand, stepped sideways and fell over a chair. While he was still off balance Brent clipped him on the jaw and the blow sounded like an axe on a log. Shotgun let out a roar, staggered back against the wall and this time he succeeded in yanking his Colt. Brent kicked viciously and his foot caught Shotgun on the forearm and sent the gun flying.

Cuthbert charged then, and his charge was like that of a bull. His left arm cut the air in powerful swings; he could not swing with his crippled right, but he used it for an uppercut which, had it landed, would have settled the thing then and there. It did not land. It wasn't skill which enabled Brent to avoid it, but sheer instinct. He ducked low and the rushing Cuthbert fell over him and went sprawling. Brent wheeled and leaped on him.

He probably would have killed the man if they hadn't pulled him off. He hadn't heard the pound of boots on the stairs, the shouts of the men who came charging up then. Hands gripped him and dragged him away and for a while he struggled desperately, his hot stare on the man who lay on the floor.

Jack Roselle's voice reached his consciousness, probably because for once Jack spoke in other than a monotone. He said, "Quit it, damn you, Tex!" and Brent tore his gaze from the prostrate Shotgun, blinked once and forced sanity back into his eyes. He said thickly, "Let me go," and when they still held him, "I said let me go! I'm all right now." They released him then.

No explanation was necessary. Judy sat huddled on the bed, the covers about her, fascinated gaze on Brent; Cuthbert lay on his back breathing hard and bleeding from the nose; Brent had bruises on his face, a cut lip and his shirt was ripped clear across the front. Two jealous men and a woman.

Cuthbert sat up and somebody helped him to his feet. He looked about dazedly, picked up his hat and put it on his head. He stood regarding Brent and there was murder in the reddish eyes. He said, "Some day I'm gonna kill you for this," and turned and stumbled through the doorway.

Jack Roselle shooed them out and Brent walked to the foot of the bed and shrugged into his coat. He picked up Shotgun's Colt and handed it to Jack, then followed Roselle into the hall without looking again at Judy. He took the key from the door, closed and locked it, drew the key and looked at Roselle. Jack was watching him with inscrutable agate eyes. He said, "You're sure hell on wheels when you get going, Tex. I'd like to have you at my back if I ever got into a jam. Be here ready to ride in the morning; we're pulling a job and I'm taking you with me."

Brent nodded and followed him downstairs. Now that it was over he was furious with himself. When he heard Judy's cry he had forgotten everything; forgotten even the task to which he had dedicated himself. There was just one redeeming feature. Jack had seen him in action and he had earned Jack's respect. Jack was taking him into his gang. It brought him that much closer to his objective and he felt better about the affair.

The ones who had preceded them into the saloon had already told what had happened upstairs and Lil was the first to meet Brent as he stepped into the room. Her rouged face was beaming, her smile was a yard wide. She said, "Good gosh and the cows come home, Tex! Don't you know you can overdo that gentleman stuff? Shotgun'll murder you, boy!"

He lifted the corner of his damaged mouth. "To hell with Shotgun; he had his chance and he muffed it. Here." He pressed the key into her hand. "When you go to bed, lock that door. If anybody bothers that kid again I'll peel that lovely hide right off of you and nail it to the back bar."

He strode down the room towards the front doors, and as he passed Lu's table he caught the hard glance she gave him. She evidently didn't like the way he championed maidens in distress. Well, he didn't either; but when a lovely girl calls on you for help, what are you going to do about it?

CHAPTER SIX

BRENT rode up to the Palace at six the next morning to find other men lounging in their saddles. They were Frisco Pete, Ed Hawley, Red Conrad and Stub Shelly. Stub's was the only name that remotely sounded like Shell and Brent had investigated him carefully only to learn that Stub was doing a stretch for manslaughter at the time his father was murdered and therefore could not be the man he sought.

From farther down the street came the thud of hoofs and six men rode by at a lope. Leading them was Shotgun Cuthbert, his favorite weapon slung by a leather thong from his saddle. He gave Brent a swift, murderous glance in passing and Brent felt the hackles rise like that of a dog. Strange how he hated the man; he had never hated anybody else like this.

Frisco Pete said, "Looks like the highway bunch is goin' on a job too." Nobody else thought it worthwhile to comment.

Jack Roselle came swinging around the corner of the Palace on his roan, leading a packhorse. He gave them a quick glance, saw that they were all there and tossed the lead rope to Stub. He said, "This way," and led them in the direction opposite to that taken by Cuthbert's gang. He glanced back and motioned with his head for Brent to join him and Brent rode up beside him.

Jack was the picture of neat efficiency. Around the Palace he wore a frock coat, striped trousers, fancy vest and a ruffled shirt; now he was dressed for the trail in dark trousers, flannel shirt, buckskin jacket and black Stetson hat. His gunbelt was hand-tooled and his .44 had pearl butt plates.

They rode steadily northward and halted at noon to cook and eat dinner. Wherever they were going Jack was in no hurry, for it was a full hour before they took to the trail again. That evening they halted by a spring, made camp and ate another good meal.

Jack had given them no information as to his plans and Brent did not question. He was a novice and would be expected to keep his mouth shut. They played poker until well after dark, then at Jack's order turned in for the night.

In the morning they started again, still at the same steady, mile-eating pace. Late in the afternoon they topped a rise and saw a town ahead of them. Jack said to Brent, "That's Franklin. We'll find a camping place a bit farther on."

Precautions against their presence being detected were taken this time. Jack led them into a wooded ravine for some distance before halting, and a fire was not kindled lest its smoke betray them. They ate a cold supper and then Jack called them about him.

"The town ahead is Franklin," he told them. "A railroad branch line runs through it and connects with the main line at Junction City, twenty miles to the north. The local which goes through Franklin at noon tomorrow will find a train waiting for it on the main line with a shipment of specie. It will be transferred to the local for delivery at Mescal, at the other end of the branch line. We're going to lift that specie."

Nobody said anything, simply nodding their understanding.

Jack went on. "Tomorrow morning before daylight we'll camp in some woods across from the station. When the train pulls in Tex and I will board the express car. The messenger will have a guard in the car with him and we will take care of them.

"At Junction City the messenger and the guard are supposed to get the specie from the main-line train. Tex and I will take their places, get the specie and put it on the local. After that it's plain sailing; we'll just ride back with the gold, join the rest of you and light out for home."

He stopped to roll and light a cigarette and now his companions became articulate. "By God, Jack, that's a pretty layout!" said Ed Hawley. Conrad said, "Foolproof, if you can run your bluff. But suppose the main-line guard decides to go back to the local with you?"

"He probably will," said Jack coolly. "Makes no difference."

Frisco Pete asked, "Why did you fetch us along? Hell, it's a two-man job."

"We'll need you. When the local pulls out of Franklin you'll circle and ride along the right-of-way until you come to a cut. When the train comes back, push some boulders on the track. The train'll have to stop and Tex and I will join you. You'll have our horses with you, of course."

They discussed the plan thoroughly. Frisco Pete said, "Mebbe some of us should ride to Junction City in case anything goes wrong at that end."

Jack shook his head. "The station there has open country all around it and there'll be armed men hanging around. The extra horses would arouse their suspicion. No, mine is the best plan. Tex and I will handle it alone."

At four in the morning they ate a cold breakfast and started out. They circled the town and daylight was breaking when they entered the strip of woods that extended clear to the right-of-way. The local was due around noon, and they spent the morning loafing, talking or sleeping. Finally Jack looked at his watch and said, "We'd better get going."

They saddled up and rode as close to the station as they dared, tied the horses and went ahead on foot. In the distance a whistle sounded. Jack and Brent stole closer to the tracks. An engine drawing an express car, a smoker and a daycoach jolted to a stop. Jack and Brent were on the side opposite the station; they walked along the train to the rear of the express car and Jack mounted the steps far enough to permit his trying the door. It was unlocked; the local was carrying nothing of value to Junction City.

When the train jerked into motion they mounted to the platform. The conductor would start taking tickets in the daycoach. When the train had picked up speed and Franklin was dropping behind them, Jack nodded and drew his gun. He opened the door of the express car and went in, and Brent followed him and closed and bolted the door behind them.

The messenger was moving express and did not glance towards them; the guard sat on a box facing the front. Jack said, "All right, boys, sit tight."

The messenger's head jerked around to stare at them; the guard tensed but otherwise did not change his position. Brent walked forward, his gun covering the messenger and Jack went up behind the guard, made him stand up and face the wall and took the heavy pistol from his belt. The messenger's gun hung on the wall near a rack containing two riot guns; Jack carried the weapons to the open doorway and dropped them outside.

The messenger said, "What is this? We ain't carrying any gold."

Jack said, "Give me your cap and strip out of those overalls."

Jack took a coil of thin rope and two gags from his shirt and handed them to Brent. When the messenger had pulled off the overalls Jack said, "Tie him up good and gag him."

When Brent had done this he fastened the man to a stanchion at the front of the car and then tied up the guard and gagged him and put him at the back of the car. The man was wearing ordinary clothing but had a uniform cap. Brent took the man's cap and put it on.

The miles sped past under clicking wheels and finally they heard the engine whistle for brakes. Jack said to Brent, "We're pulling into Junction City and I'll have to unload the express. It's the toughest part of the job. You stay out of sight and watch those two birds."

The train swerved to the right and Brent, glancing through the doorway saw that the track swept in two opposite curves to join the main line, which ran at right angles to the branch line. They were on the right hand curve and he saw that they would come out on the main line, back along it to a point beyond the switches, then move over on the left hand curve, thus turning around. The station was in the triangle formed by the tracks.

The train stopped at the station platform, a baggage truck rolled up beside the car door and Jack, wearing the messenger's cap and overalls, passed out the express and baggage to a man who never gave him a second glance. So far they were playing in luck.

The train moved on to the main line, backed, then jolted forward on the other side of the triangle of track, pulled past the station and halted by a water tank beyond the station. The main-line train was waiting. Jack and Brent descended the short iron ladder steps to the ground; walked to the station platform, mounted it and went boldly past the building. There was a hand truck leaning against the wall and Jack calmly took it and rolled it ahead of him.

They followed a path which paralleled the right-of-way, passing the coaches of the main-line train and approaching the express car. Its door was open and two men stood in the entrance. Both had guns strapped about them. Jack dropped the handles of the truck and said, "All right; pass it down."

The messenger asked, "You Charles Benson?"

"That's right. Want me to sign for it?"

The messenger passed down a book and a pencil and Jack boldly wrote the name Charles Benson and handed it back. The messenger pushed an ironbound box to the door and Jack lifted it down and put it onto the truck. The messenger started to descend the ladder and Jack straightened and said, "You fellows needn't come along; the coast looks clear."

"We go along just the same," said the messenger. "You know the orders."

The guard followed him down and Jack picked up the handles of the truck and started wheeling it towards the local. The messenger walked a couple feet behind him and a bit to his right; the guard was the same distance behind him and to the left. Brent followed.

They passed the station safely, came to the daycoach of the

local. Only the smoker to pass, and they would be at the express car. And then as they were about to pass the platform of the smoker the conductor came down its steps and glanced at them. Brent saw puzzlement come into his eyes, then sudden suspicion. He blurted, "Hey! You ain't Charley Benson! Where is he?"

Jack started pushing the truck faster. The messenger stopped suddenly, his hand falling to the butt of his gun. He called, "Hey, you! Halt or I'll fire!"

Brent drew his gun, took one step forward and brought the seven-and-one-half-inch barrel down on the fellow's head. He slumped to the ground like a wet sack. Brent pivoted to his left; the guard had snatched out his gun and was whirling. Brent shot the fellow through the forearm and he dropped the gun and grabbed his maimed wrist. The conductor stood rooted, staring.

Brent snatched up the gun the guard had dropped, made a menacing motion with it, said, "Get going!" and fired into the ground to lend the man speed. The fellow took off at a run, still clinging to his arm.

Back at the station, a hundred yards off, three men came running out of the building. Two of them had rifles and they started shooting as they ran. The bullets came close. Up ahead the fireman still stood on the tender; the engineer was climbing down from the cab. Jack had dropped the handles of the truck and had drawn his gun. Brent yelled, "Put that box inside!"

"We got to get out of here!" Jack shouted back.

"Put it inside, I tell you!" Brent turned to the conductor. "Come along with me." He herded the man along the side of the smoker and at its front end he said, "Uncouple the express car." The conductor stepped between the cars and pulled the coupling pin. "Now beat it," ordered Brent.

Lead was whistling by him, but the marksmen were running and did not dare to draw down too fine because of the proximity of the conductor and the engineer. Jack was pushing the specie box into the express car; he glanced questioningly at Brent as the latter ran by. Brent passed him, flourished his guns at the engineer and said, "Back into the cab and get this thing rolling!"

He climbed the steps behind the engineer, stood on the gangway, his guns raised. He grated, "Open that throttle! You on the tender, get down here and keep that fire going!"

The engine started with a jolt, taking the express car with it. Brent heard the sound of gunfire from the express car and knew that Jack had gone into action. The engine picked up speed and the sound of firing died away.

They made fast time, knowing that it would be a matter of minutes only until the main-line train would be switched to the branch line to follow them with a quickly gathered posse. Less than twenty minutes later the engineer closed the throttle and reversed. "Something on the track!" he shouted. The wheels grated on the rails and they slid to a stop twenty feet from several boulders which lay across the track. Behind them Brent heard the frantic whistle of the pursuing train.

Around the far end of the cut came four horsemen. Two of them led saddled horses and a third had a pack horse in tow. The one with Brent's horse halted beside the cab, his gun covering the engine crew. He said, "Okay, Tex, hop on," and Brent stepped into his saddle.

The others had gone to the express car and were working like Trojans, spurred by the sounds of pursuit. Jack passed out the specie box and it was lashed on the pack saddle. Jack snatched up his and Brent's hat and leaped on his own horse and the whole party circled around the express car and cut for the open range. Brent tossed away the guard's cap and took his hat from Jack. In the near distance the pursuing train vomited its smoke into the sky.

Jack shouted, "Straight for the hills and cover. Then we'll circle."

Frisco Pete was leading; he turned to grin at them. "Pretty close, huh? You fellers sure did a sweet job."

Jack spoke to Brent above the pound of hoofs. "I guess I had the right hunch when I picked you to come along. Stick with me, Tex, and you'll go a long way."

It came to Brent then that perhaps the answer to his problem lay in becoming a leader of one of the gangs. The idea took root and grew, its possibilities rocking him. If he could achieve that goal he must eventually come face to face with the man who led these wild outlaw bands, the man who had murdered his father and his brother!

CHAPTER SEVEN

THEY rode into Destiny around suppertime of the second day, but Jack did not accompany them into town. A short distance from Destiny he took the pack horse with its burden of specie and left them, saying he'd see them later. Brent guessed that he was going to hide the gold and, if he himself were not the leader, report to the person who was. Brent would have liked to follow him, but there was nothing at all he could do about it.

He put his horse in the livery corral and walked to the Chinese restaurant for his supper. Judy and Lil were just coming out and the latter hailed him with her usual, "Hi-yuh, Tex!" and Judy gave him her warmest smile. Lil asked if the hunting had been good and he answered that it was.

"I'm so glad you got back safely, Tex," said Judy. "I haven't had a chance to thank you for what you did the other night."

"It was a real pleasure, Judy. I just don't like Shotgun Cuthbert."

They went on up the street and Brent entered the restaurant, ate his supper, then went out and prowled about the town. He looked in the saloons and stores for Biff Williams and did not find him, nor was he in the shack where he hung out. His absence might mean that he had gone to meet Jack and receive his report, in which case it would seem that he was the man Brent sought. There was nothing conclusive about this and the thing remained a riddle.

Brent finally entered the Palace, tilted a chair against the wall and sat down. Things were stirring now and he saw Judy and Lil at a table with a couple of outlaws. He had a hunch that Lil was looking out for Judy and was thankful for it.

Lu Roselle came in comparatively early, for with Jack gone she was boss of the place. Brent, gazing at her, had to admit that she was stunning. Her green evening gown was just tight enough in the right places, her coppery hair was brushed and glinting, her makeup was perfect and accentuated the sultriness of the green eyes.

He still believed that she was the key to the mystery he was trying to solve; Jack knew the identity of the unknown leader and he would confide in her if he confided in anybody. He got up and sauntered about the room, finally dropping into a chair at her table. The green eyes were cool and impersonal when she turned them on him, so he gave her his lopsided grin and said, "Lu, you sure look swell tonight."

"It's a wonder you noticed it with that Judy girl in the room."

He raised his left eyebrow. "You're thinking of the other night but you've got it wrong. I don't like Shotgun Cuthbert and his sneaking upstairs gave me an excuse to tangle with him."

She must have believed him for her lips curved in a smile. "If that's the case I'll let you buy me a drink."

He signaled the bartender and she said in a low voice, "Jack's out of town. If you'd like to drop in for a drink I could leave the back door unlocked."

"That'd be right risky, wouldn't it?"

"Not if you're careful."

The bartender brought their drinks and they were silent until he had gone. He said, "If Jack finds out you'll be in bad with him."

"I'm willing to take the chance if you are." The green eyes challenged him.

He said shortly, "I'll be there. Here's how!"

They drank and he got up and moved away from her table. He was watching for Biff Williams to appear, but the hours drifted by and Biff did not come in. After a while he got up and went out to make another circuit of the town. He located Biff in another saloon playing poker with three of his gang, but how long he had been there Brent had no way of learning.

He returned to the Palace in time to hear Judy sing, felt an unreasonable anger stir him when she was surrounded by men after she had finished, and was making his way towards the door when Cliff Durham entered. Cliff's face darkened at sight of Brent and he halted in a narrow space where Brent could not pass. Brent asked, "Find that fellow you're looking for?"

"Not yet, but I will. Funny thing; that hoss of yours wears the same size shoe as the one I'm lookin' for."

"So do thousands of others; it's a standard size."

"Uh-huh, but I got a good look at a whole set of prints on the bank of a creek back in the hills and I made tracings of them and compared them with the prints of your hoss. Matched exactly."

"So you're going to arrest me for what this fellow did, huh?"

"No. No, I ain't aimin' to arrest you. You see, that bruise you see on my face wasn't made by no hoss like I told you. Some feller kicked me when I was down and layin' on my back. When I find out for sure who it was I'm goin' to walk up to him and put a slug into his belly."

"I bet," drawled Brent, "that when you were a boy your idea of fun was to pull legs and wings off bugs. Now move your carcass; I'm on the way out."

Cliff eyed him hard for a moment longer, then stepped aside. Brent went out, decided it was a good time to evade the marshal and circled to the alley and walked to Jack Roselle's house. He went into the stable and waited there until he heard the faint click of Lu's heels on the plank sidewalk, then crossed to the back door and was standing in the shadows when she unlocked the door. He slipped inside, said hello, and she said, "Wait until I pull down the shades in the living room."

When he finally joined her she came readily to his arms and he held her close and kissed her. It was not hard to do; she was a lovely woman and knew all the tricks of the trade. They walked to the cabinet and he stood with an arm around her while she poured drinks for them. They took glasses and walked to the divan, and he drew her down beside him. She cuddled up to him and he caught the subtle fragrance of her hair. He said, "You're like a rose, Lu; you smell as sweet as you look."

The green eyes looked up at him, narrowed like those of a pleased kitten. She murmured, "That was sweet, Tex." She raised her glass, "Luck!"

"Plenty of it," he said fervently, knowing he'd need it.

"Another?"

"Not right now." His arm was about her and he glanced about as though apprehensive. "You're sure Jack won't walk in on us?"

"Of course I'm sure."

"I'd feel safer if you'd tell me where he is."

"If I did and he found it out he'd probably kill me."

"His sister?"

"His own mother. Jack hates a double-crosser."

"That's what's worrying me."

"I thought you weren't afraid of him."

"Honey, I'm afraid of anybody who's apt to walk up on me

and sock a slug into me without advance notice. Is this the regular routine, to cache the loot after a raid? Do all the gang leaders do it?" He tried to sound unconcerned.

"Uh-huh." She had put her head on his shoulder and the green eyes were closed. "They have to—" She broke off abruptly.

She opened her eyes. "They have to make sure that there's nothing in town to give them away if they should be followed."

He had caught her off guard and she had come near to making a break. He was sure she had been about to say that the leaders had to report to—somebody.

"I have a hunch that Jack plans the jobs for all three gangs."

"What makes you think that?" There was a hint of suspicion in the question.

"The way the gangs work. They never conflict and each outfit sticks to one branch of the business. It looks as though one man is directing and Jack's the natural choice."

"Bright boy! Keep right on guessing if it amuses you."

"I'm just curious. Do they have regular times for splitting the loot?"

"You'll get your share when the time comes." She pulled away from him to regard him through narrowed lids. "What is this? Are you trying to pump me?"

He drew her to him and kissed her. "Just like to hear myself talk." He glanced at the windows. "You sure those shades are all the way down?"

"Yes, I'm sure." She said it a bit scornfully. "You know, you're not half the hero I thought you were."

"I keep thinking of Cliff Durham; he'd sure like to catch me in something."

"You and me both, darling. For some reason he's been trying to get the goods on me ever since they made him marshal."

He wanted to ask her when that was but didn't dare quiz her any more. If she thought he were fishing for information she'd betray him in a minute to Jack Roselle. Somewhere along the line his brother Cole had made a slip and he must be careful not to repeat the mistake.

He put aside his questions for a more opportune moment and gave her his whole attention. He knew that she was shallow and vain and that she was entertaining him because he had played hard to get. Well, if she had information that he needed he would pry it out of her if it were at all possible.

An hour later he told her he had to go. "Cliff will be wondering about the light in the house; he'll sneak up and find the shades drawn and then he'll hide somewhere to see who comes out."

"I could put out the light and raise the shades," she suggested.

"No dice," he said with assumed regret. "I'd better go before I spoil a good thing."

She sighed. "Maybe you're right; but it may be a long time before we have another chance to be together."

He got up and she rose with him. Once more he held her, finding it quite agreeable but somehow wishing it were Judy in his arms. He told her goodnight with all the fervor of a devoted lover and made his way to his shack, his problem still unsolved.

He slept late and killed time the following day. Ever mindful that his horse must always be in firstclass shape he fitted new shoes all around and groomed the animal until he shone. He deliberately waited until after the girls had eaten before going to the restaurant for supper. He was aware of a growing desire to be near Judy and resented it; one woman was complication enough when a man's life hung by such a thin thread as did his.

It was still fairly early when he went to the Palace, but Jack was back at his accustomed place at the end of the bar. Uncle Jim Ferguson had returned from his gold buying trip and was at the bar. Biff Williams sat at a table with Judy, and Bub Whittaker, the Cockeyed Kid, slept in a tilted chair with his hat drawn over his eyes. Lu Roselle had not yet come in.

Brent sauntered to the bar, exchanged a casual word with Jack and ordered a drink. He was toying with the glass when hoofbeats sounded outside and a moment later the swinging doors parted to admit three men. Brent recognized them as members of Shotgun's highway bunch. They walked stiffly as though weary from hard riding and their faces were pinched and grim. They went to the bar and called for drinks.

A hush fell over the place; something had gone wrong and every person in the Palace sensed it. Jack walked along the bar, his agate eyes on them. He said, "Drinks on the house, boys. Looks like you ran into trouble."

One of them said, "You're damned right we ran into trouble. Shotgun and Gleason are bein' patched up by the doc; Kaintuck won't be back. They drilled him plumb through the head."

They drank and Jack said, "Have another and tell us about it."

"Ain't a lot to tell. We stopped the stage where we was supposed to. The guard grabbed up his gun and Shotgun blasted

45

hell out of him. Gave him both barrels. If we'd took the specie box and lit out everything woulda been jake, but Shotgun figgered we might collect a little extry from the passengers. It was a mistake. We lined 'em up by the side of the road and Shotgun started goin' through 'em when they hit us.

"There was a posse followin' the stage. A bend in the trail kept us from seein' them and Shotgun hadn't sent anybody back to watch. They heard that scattergun of his'n and come ridin' around the bend and started shootin' before we could get to our hosses. Kaintuck got it right off and Shotgun and Gleason while we was runnin' for the hosses. Gleason was drilled through the hip and Shotgun got a busted arm."

Jack asked in his toneless voice, "Get the specie?"

"Hell, no! All we got was out of there. I tell you, Jack, it's a wonder more of us wasn't killed. They follered us for miles before we finally shook 'em; hadda make a big circle to lead 'em away from Destiny. But our hosses were rested and that told in the end."

Brent experienced a thrill of satisfaction; he had no sympathy at all for these outlaws, and the thought that Shotgun had fallen down on the job pleased him. There was a chance now that another would be chosen to fill his place and perhaps if Jack spoke up for him, Brent might be that man. Anticipation sent the blood racing through his veins. His selection would mean that at long last he would meet the man he wanted so much to meet. And when he met him he was more than ever convinced he would be meeting the murderer of his father and his brother.

CHAPTER EIGHT

BIFF WILLIAMS and his gang rode away the next morning. Their departure told Brent that despite his careful watching Biff had contacted the unknown leader and had been given his instructions.

That evening Brent met Judy and Lil at the restaurant and once more ate supper with them. He noticed at once that

Judy's face was free of the strained look which had been present ever since her first night at the Palace. The sparkle had returned to her eyes and she chatted gaily.

He said, "You must be getting used to the life, Judy; you act like you're really enjoying it."

Lil said, "It ain't that, Tex; it's just that with Biff's two hands gone and one of Shotgun's in a sling the kid has to put up with only a fourth as many pawin's. All she needs now is for Lu Roselle to sprain her tongue or get smallpox or somethin'."

"So Lu's been riding you."

"Yes," answered Judy. "For some reason she doesn't like me. Sometimes I think—" she looked doubtfully at him—"it's because you stood up for me. Tex, I hope I haven't caused any trouble between you."

"Between me and Lu? You haven't. I hardly know her. She's probably sore because you have something she hasn't. You're fresh and unspoiled and a lot prettier than she is or ever will be."

Judy's eyes shone and she put a hand impulsively over his. "Honest, Tex, do you think so?"

He looked deep into the warm brown eyes. "I told you once, I'll tell you again. I think you're the sweetest kid God ever put on earth."

Their glances held and it was as though they were looking into each other's souls. Lil eyed them shrewdly, her gaze going swiftly from Tex to Judy and then back again. She said, "If you two kids are in love the best thing for you to do is get the hell out of Destiny."

With a conscious effort, Brent regained control of his emotions. In love? Never in a million years. There was no room in his heart for love until he had squared the debt he owed his father and Cole. He withdrew his hand and his face hardened. "You're loco, Lil," he said shortly. "I can't afford to fall in love with any woman. I'm an outlaw; I can't dodge handcuffs and rolling pins at the same time. But I agree with you that Judy should get out of Destiny."

"Where would I go?" asked Judy quietly. "I have no home, no friends out here and none back East that I'd want to go to."

"You could get out of Destiny, go to some town where you could find decent work."

He felt her intent gaze upon him and refused to meet it. At last she said, "No. I'll stay here. One just can't run from— Destiny."

Brent did not walk back to the Palace with them. Somehow when he was with Judy he was inclined to forget the purpose which had brought him to Destiny and there were moments like that in the restaurant when she had put her hand over his that he faltered in his determination to see the business through to the bitter end.

The evening passed without incident. With Biff gone and Shotgun nursing a broken arm, Judy was freed of the strain she felt whenever they were present. She sang more gaily and laughed a lot; Uncle Jim Ferguson seemed to delight in sitting at a table with her drinking beer. She drank carefully and Brent guessed that when somebody ordered hard liquor she was being served tea. Cliff Durham was in and out of the place and Brent felt sure the marshal was checking on him, hoping to catch him wearing a black robe and in the act of robbing a store.

It was the next evening that he cemented his friendship with Bub Whittaker, the Cockeyed Kid. He had lingered at the Palace in order to avoid having supper with Judy and Lil, and the place was nearly empty. Bub was in a chair against the wall looking forlorn, and Brent beckoned him over to the bar and ordered a drink for him. He noticed that Bub's fingers shook when he seized the glass. Bub downed the liquor and said, "Thank-ee, Tex, you're shore a good man and some day I'm gonna repay you. Uncle Jim's back and tomorry he'll give me four bits for sweepin' out his office."

"I wondered what you did for a living, Bub. Thought maybe you had a roll cached away from the old days."

Bub shook his head. "That's the trouble with the owlhoot trail; you throw it away as fast as you gather it. Me, I've made two fortunes and spent three. Now they say I'm too old to j'in up with any of the outfits and I jest putter around with odd jobs."

Brent eyed him narrowly. The old man's face looked thin and pinched. He asked casually, "Had your supper yet?"

"Wal, no. But I ain't a bit hongry, Tex; I'll eat later mebbe."

"I was sort of hoping you'd keep me company. I'm about ready to go up to the restaurant and wrap myself around one of those tenderloin steaks." He raised his glass, his gaze on the old man's reflection in the mirror. He saw Bub wince.

"Thank-ee, Tex, but I aim to eat sorta light tonight."

"Aw, come along. The meal's on me this time. You can buy me one when your ship comes in." He took the old man's arm and steered him towards the doorway. They went up the street together and went into the restaurant and Brent ordered for both of them. The Cockeyed Kid said, "You know, Tex, I'm swallerin' a heap of pride lettin' you buy me this here meal. Drinks is different, but I'm used to payin' for my own grub. Only way I can square things with m' conscience is by rememberin' that I done you a little favor t'other night."

"The other night?" Brent frowned, trying to recall when the old fellow had done him a favor. It came at him at last. "Mean to tell me those three nines weren't just an accident?"

"Whadda you think I spilled the deck on the floor for?"

"Why, you old catamount! Don't you ever talk about paying me back for a few drinks and a meal."

"Hell, I'd do a heap more for you if I got the chanct. You ever git into a jam you come to me; I ain't much on looks but I can still sling a six with the best of 'em and don't you think I can't."

Whittaker ate like a starving man and Brent was filled with a strange pity for the old fellow. When at last Bub sighed and pushed back his plate Brent said, "You ought to eat more regular. I'm going to stake you to ten bucks until you get straightened out and I don't want any objections." He pressed a gold piece into Bub's hand.

Bub glared at him, or at least Brent thought that was what he was doing, although he couldn't be sure just where the crossed eyes were looking. "Now looky here, Tex; I ain't takin' no handouts. I'll pay my own way."

"Sure you will. Some day you're going to pay me back. Some day I may need a friend and need him bad. If you mean what you said about helping me I'll want you to be fat and sassy and not half-starved and weak."

Bub's face tightened. "All right, I'll take it; but only on the condition that you call me when you need that extry gun. Shake on it!"

Brent shook hands solemnly, never dreaming that he would ever call upon Bub to keep his promise of aid.

It was the third evening after Biff's departure that the stranger appeared. He came into the Palace, walked to the bar and bought a drink and there was an instant stopping of conversation. When men resumed talking the topics were general ones with no reference to raids or holdups. The stranger finished his drink, wandered about gambling a few dollars away, then found a chair, tilted it against the wall and proceeded to go to sleep.

At a low-voiced order from Jack, Brent went out and looked the man's horse over, then unstrapped the blanket roll, carried it back to the Palace stable, lighted a lantern and went through it carefully. It contained no clue to the stranger's identity, held only the customary necessities of a horseman on a long trip. Brent rolled it up as it had been, replaced it and reported his failure to find anything significant. When the stranger finally left, Frisco Pete followed him and returned to inform them that the man had staked out his horse and made camp a short distance from town.

Biff's men returned from their raid in the daytime, and Brent did not learn of it until that evening; consequently, he had no chance to check on Jack and Shotgun. Biff might have met either of them during the day. Biff came into the Palace that night and had evidently been tipped off to the presence of the stranger, for he said nothing about the job; but there was a smug complacency about him that bespoke success.

As the evening passed Biff drank pretty heavily and presently Brent saw him watching Judy and knew there was trouble for the girl in the offing. The man was big and strong and used to taking what he wanted, and right now he wanted Judy. A slow anger kindled within Brent, and he stifled it determinedly. He didn't want to tangle with Biff over the girl, but at the same time her very helplessness appealed to him. She was alone, friendless and utterly dependent upon herself. And she was decent too, he knew; the Palace was no place for her. He walked over to her table, said, "May I?" and when she smiled and nodded raised his fingers to the bartender in a signal for drinks.

She said, "This is an unexpected pleasure, Tex. I was afraid you'd forgotten me."

"I couldn't do that, Judy." He had taken a chair which allowed him to watch Biff, and he knew from Biff's expression that the man was not pleased.

The bartender brought their drinks and they toasted each other and he asked politely, "Tea?" She said, "Yes. I like it so much better, even though it's costing you as much as whiskey."

He wanted to kill time, to hold her with him. He said, "Tell me about yourself, Judy, won't you?"

She began talking and he listened, making an occasional remark, keeping one eye on the restless Williams, ordering drinks at appropriate intervals. Biff became increasingly impatient and finally Brent knew the break was coming. Williams tossed off a whiskey, thumped the glass on the bar and came striding purposefully towards the table. Brent watched, appearing not to do so. Judy broke off in the middle of the sentence and tensed, and he saw apprehension and fear come into her face. Still he did not look at Williams.

A big rough hand bit into his shoulder and then he looked up. Biff glared down at him, said gruffly, "You've been here long enough, Tex. Give somebody else a chance."

Brent drawled, "I don't know about that, Biff."

"I do. I been gone four days; you've had your chance." The hand was like an iron clamp and Brent was helpless while he was seated.

He got up slowly and the hand was removed. He said, still drawling, "That's one way of looking at it, but it's not my way. And I don't like big, heavy hands on my shoulders."

"You don't, huh? Well, then, I'll put it somewhere else."

They were standing less than two feet apart, facing each other, and Biff's movement was lightning fast. His right fist came up in a powerful uppercut aimed at the point of Brent's chin and all the power of his solid heavy frame was behind the blow. Brent, knowing that something like this must come, jerked his head aside and Biff's knuckles raked across his cheek with a force that sent him staggering sideways; but even as he moved he sank a short left to the pit of Biff's stomach and heard the gasp of agony that was forced from the big man's lips.

Brent caught his balance with his weight on his right foot, thrust towards Williams with all the power of his leg muscles and crossed a hard right to the side of Biff's jaw. Williams stumbled and fell over the next table; the legs gave under his great weight and he went down on top of it. Brent's gun whipped out and covered him even as he grabbed for his own Colt. Brent drawled, "I reckon you'd better not try it, Biff."

He saw three of Biff's men coming at a fast walk, saw Frisco Pete and Red Conrad detach themselves from the bar to follow them. Frisco Pete said, "They don't need no help, boys," and the three slowed down, flashed backward glances and kept their hands away from their hardware.

Williams was lying on the wreck of the table supporting himself with an arm. His face, which had whitened with anger, slowly turned a dull red. He got up slowly and Brent took a backward step to give him room.

Jack Roselle came over from the end of the bar and said in his toneless voice, "What's the trouble, Tex?"

"No trouble, Jack. Biff got a little impatient because I was buying drinks for Judy and offered to relieve me. I didn't want to be relieved. I had an idea that as long as I spend money I can sit with whoever I choose and as long as I want to. Maybe I'm wrong."

"No, you're not wrong." He turned to Biff. "Plenty other girls on the floor, Biff. And plenty more nights coming up. You socked Tex and he socked you; that ends it as far as the Palace is concerned. Come over and have a drink."

Biff stood there glaring, but he had no defense and he knew it. Had his first blow landed, the fight would have ended differently. But it hadn't. He looked about him, saw that his men were outnumbered and that the sympathy of the crowd was with Tex, and accepted temporary defeat. He said, "Yeah, there are other nights comin'." He looked at Judy, sitting white-faced and staring at the table. "I aim to make you remember at least one of them."

He turned away and walked with Jack to the bar.

Brent holstered his gun, signaled the bartender for drinks, and calmly sat down. "Let's see," he said. "You were telling me how you came to join up with Sam Carter's outfit. Go on from there."

CHAPTER NINE

BIFF left shortly thereafter but Brent remained at the table with Judy until Ferguson came over and smiled down at them. Uncle Jim said, "Do you feel like being relieved now? I'd be glad to take over."

Brent willingly surrendered his place and went away with the memory of Judy's tremulous smile.

Although he had been watching Biff, not a word of Judy's recital had escaped him. It was a story that stirred him, the story of a girl who'd lost both parents in childhood and had been reared by relatives who looked upon the task as an obligation they could not escape. As soon as she was able to she had gone to work; she worked in stores and finally in a florist's shop. It was here that Sam Carter had met her and had urged her to join his troupe.

Judy had read of the West, its vastness, its wildness, its hospitality and the opportunities it offered those who were not afraid to gamble. She had gambled and had ended in the Palace; but she had loved the country from the very first and she was determined to stay.

He admired her for her courage and at the same time was appalled at what might lie ahead of her. When he had asked her about this she had said, "While my father and mother were alive they taught me to be good and I've never forgotten their lessons. I took this job because it was the only one I could get, but I'm going to save my commissions until I have enough to leave Destiny with my chin in the air."

And suddenly he realized what he had known all along but was too stubborn to admit. He loved Judy Clane. If Providence spared his life and the law spared him his liberty he'd leave with her and they'd win their way together in this West they both loved. And having made the decision, he pushed thoughts of a rosy future to the back of his mind and concentrated once more on the immediate task.

Lu ignored him the rest of the evening. She must have guessed by this time that if not actually in love with Judy he was strongly attracted, and the knowledge that any of her girls could be more fascinating than herself would have hurt her vanity. He didn't much care; if she had any information worthwhile she was canny enough or scared enough to keep it to herself.

He went home when the Palace closed, sensed that he was being followed and, thinking that the stalker might be Biff, ducked into a passageway and waited until the man passed. The fellow was as broad as was Williams but not as tall. It was Destiny's marshal, Cliff Durham, still hopeful of catching Brent in a black robe.

Brent in turn followed Durham and saw him blend with the shadows of a tree across from the shack. As he passed, Brent said cheerfully, "Nice evening to be out, isn't it, Cliff?" and got no answer.

He slept late and killed time during the day by playing cards in one of the saloons. This was the monotonous part of an outlaw's life, the period of stagnation between raids. It was all the more irksome because he could not check on his suspects during the daytime. He killed the desire to be with Judy at the restaurant, and deliberately waited until the girls had eaten and returned to the Palace. When he finally entered the place himself, things were in full swing.

Biff and Shotgun were at the bar but not together. A truce existed between Brent and Shotgun, a truce that both men took for granted would last until Shotgun's arm had healed. Then it would be a shootout; there was no doubt about it. There would be another encounter with Williams, the time and place to be selected by Biff. There was no doubt of that either. Men of his caliber and standing could not afford to take a beating without handing out a bigger and better one in return; but Brent was sure that as long as he kept clear of Williams, Jack would not permit the encounter to take place in the Palace.

The stranger was also at the bar and Brent took a place beside him, nodded a greeting and said, "Have a drink?"

"I'm buyin' you one," answered the man and beckoned to the bartender.

They raised their glasses and drank and the stranger asked, "How does a feller go about gettin' a job in this town?"

"Depends upon the job."

"I ain't particular, providin' it pays good and there ain't too much work."

"That lets out cowpunching. You might try prospecting."

"Too slow. I like to gather gold fast." He added significantly, "I'm pretty good with a six-gun and I don't run easy."

"Stick around and something might turn up." Brent was interested in the man; nobody seemed to know him, but Jack had talked with him and there was always the possibility that the fellow's name was Shell.

"They call me Tex," Brent volunteered.

"Pleased to meetcha. I'm Lem Purdy."

Brent bought a drink and said, "See you later, Lem," and walked away. He made a circuit of the room, then stopped at the end of the bar and borrowed a match from Jack. He said, "The pilgrim's name is Lem Purdy and he's looking for a job that pays a lot for a little. Says he can shoot."

Jack nodded. "Keep your mouth buttoned until I pass the word."

Brent lighted a cigarette. "Want to do me a favor?"

"What is it?" There was no promise in the flat voice.

"Tell that sister of yours to lay off Judy Clane."

"Why should I?"

"Because she's had tough luck, and I like her and want her to get a break."

"I'll tell her."

Brent walked away, saw the Cockeyed Kid on the far side of the room and took a chair beside him. "How's the bankroll holding out, Bub?"

"I'm fattenin' up. I'll be ready when you need me."

Ferguson was at the roulette table and after a while he saw Brent and came over to sit beside him. "Luck ran out on me," he said dolefully. "Figured I'd better lay off before they break me. Tex, it tickled me to see you keep Judy away from Biff, but you've made yourself a bad enemy. And you can't keep him away from the girl indefinitely."

Jack Roselle nodded to the bartender who played the piano and he went over and said something to Judy. She got up and jumped lightly to the stage. The bartender sat down at the piano and immediately there was a concerted move towards the platform. Brent drifted along with the rest and dropped into a chair at Lu's table. Judy began to sing.

Lu said in a sharp whisper, "You louse!"

"Me? Thanks; same to you."

"Why did you fight with Biff over that girl? God knows you had her to yourself long enough."

"He went about getting her the wrong way, and my money's just as good as his."

"Spend some of it on the other girls. Judy's getting too damned choosey."

"Maybe it's me that's choosey. Now hush up; I want to listen."

Lu plumped around in her chair and gave him a fine view of smooth white shoulders and quite a bit of back. He wanted it that way.

Judy never sang better, and she sang most of her songs directly to him. She seemed to have lost her fear and he had the feeling that she was deliberately taunting Lu Roselle. Lu squirmed in her chair and her green eyes blazed hate across the distance which separated them.

When she had finished her act, Judy was surrounded by men. She joked with them, parried their passes skillfully and managed to keep them in a good humor. She got away from them at last and sat down at a table with Red Conrad. They drank and Red leaned across the table and said something to her. Brent saw her shake her head. Lu got up from her table, went over and spoke to Judy; Judy looked up at her and Brent saw her lips frame a blunt *no*.

Ferguson was sitting beside Brent and he also was watching Judy's table. He said, "I'm going to talk with Lu." He went across the room, took Lu by an arm and drew her away from Judy's table. She didn't want to leave but he was insistent and she finally accompanied him to her own table and sat down. Ferguson called for drinks and started talking to her. He certainly had a way about him, this man they called Uncle Jim, for presently the tight look left Lu's face and she smiled slightly.

When their drink was served, Ferguson got up and crossed to where Judy and Red were sitting. He spoke to them and they got up and moved over to Lu's table. Ferguson called for another round of drinks and Lu went to the bar and fetched them herself. The four drank and Lu called for a round. Judy was laughing and talking and Brent's eyes narrowed slightly. He hoped she wasn't going to repeat her performance of the first night. He glanced over at the bar; Biff and Shotgun had turned and were watching the party.

Red Conrad bought a round and again Lu brought the drinks from the bar. Ferguson shook his head in refusal, then changed his mind and drank. He got up, waved a big hand in farewell, patted Lu on the shoulder and ambled over to where Brent stood by the faro layout. He was smiling broadly. He took Brent by an arm and whispered, "I think I got things fixed up. The lion and the lamb are—well, not lying down together but drinking together, which is just as good. The pace is getting too fast for me; I'm going home and turn in." He clapped Brent on the shoulder. "Everything'll be all right now."

"Is Judy drinking tea or whiskey?"

"Only one whiskey; the others, by her expression, were tea. Don't worry; she's learned her lesson."

He went out, waving farewell to the men who wished him goodnight.

With his departure the gaiety at Lu's table quickly died. After a while Red got up, said a somewhat blurred goodnight and wove along the aisle between layouts and bar and through the front door to the street. Brent guessed that Red felt the need for air. Judy sat silent, a bit rigid, staring across the table. Brent saw her blink her eyes, then shake her head. She said something to Lu and got unsteadily to her feet. Brent moved past the blackjack table and got close enough to hear Lu say, "What's the matter with you? Drunk again?"

Judy shook her head, "Just—sleepy. I'm so—sleepy."

"Then go upstairs and go to bed." Lu called, "Lil!" and when Lil came over she said, "Judy's going to sleep standing up. Take her to her room and put her to bed."

"Sure. Come on, kid, let's go." She took Judy by an arm and they walked to the doorway in the wall and Jack, watching them with agate eyes, opened the door for them and closed it after they had gone. He crossed to Lu and asked her something and Brent heard her answer, "Says she's just sleepy. She only had one whiskey, and if she can get drunk on cold tea she'd better go back to the nursery."

Brent glanced across the room at Biff Williams. He had stepped back from the bar and was watching the doorway through which the girls had gone. He turned suddenly and went out to the street; Brent, his face tightening, followed him.

Biff went down the street and turned into another saloon, and Brent walked up to the half door and looked over them. Biff was at the bar. He had a drink then walked over to where four of his men were seated about a poker table. He said something and then sat down with them. Brent moved away into

56

the shadows, leaned against the wall and smoked a cigarette. Presently a better idea occurred to him and he walked past the saloon, glancing over the doors to be sure Biff was still there, then turned into the alley and followed it to the rear of the Palace. The door was open and he could see the stairs. He settled down in the dark where he could see anybody who might enter from the rear or by the side door.

An hour passed; nobody entered the outside doorway or came through to the stairs from the saloon, and nobody came out. He walked around the block and went into the Palace through the front entrance. Biff had not returned, and Shotgun was not in sight. Brent found Lil at the back of the room and asked, "Was Judy all right when you took her upstairs?"

"I guess so. I put her to bed and left her. She went right to sleep."

"What made her so sleepy all of a sudden?"

"Tex, I'm wonderin' about that myself. I smelled her breath and it had a sort of funny smell. You know, not all whiskey; somethin' else mixed in."

"Come upstairs with me and we'll see if she's all right."

Lil gave him a startled look. His face had tightened and his eyes were narrowed. She said, "Sure, Tex."

They went upstairs together and Lil tried the door. It was locked. She turned a puzzled face to Brent. "That's funny. I left her sleepin' sound! how could the door get locked?"

Brent rapped on the door. "Judy! You awake?"

They heard soft sounds in the room as though somebody was moving about in the darkness, then came a distinct thump as the person stumbled over a chair. Brent rapped again. "Judy! Open up!"

There came another soft thump, then a slithering sound followed by a more distant thud. Judy did not answer.

Lil said, "Tex, somethin's wrong!" Her voice was tense with anxiety.

He stepped back, hunched his shoulders and hit the door like a battering ram. The lock gave at the impact and the door flew open. The light from the hall was too dim to show him much; he thumbed a match into flame and held it high.

Judy lay asleep on the bed, partly uncovered, her dark hair streaming over the pillow. She was breathing deeply and regularly. Lil said, "She seems to be all right, but somebody's been messin' with the bedcovers."

Brent struck another match and lighted the lamp on the washstand. He came back to the bed, bent over Judy and smelled her breath, then raised an eyelid and looked at the pupil. He said softly, slowly, "The dirty bum."

He straightened and looked about the room. The window was open; he crossed to it and saw that it overlooked the roof of the adjoining building. He knew now why he had seen nobody come or go through the back doorway. Lil said, "What is it, Tex?"

He turned and she saw the fury in his face. "Laudanum," he said briefly. "Her drink was doped. And it looks as though we got here just in time."

CHAPTER TEN

Brent said to Lil, "Stay here with her. I'll fix it with Jack."

He went out of the room, down the stairs and into the saloon. He went to Jack and said, "Somebody doped Judy and got through the window into her room. We scared him off when we tried to get in. I told Lil to stay with her."

Jack nodded and said nothing. There was nothing to say.

Brent went over to Lu's table and asked shortly, "Who told you to put laudanum in Judy's drink?"

"Did somebody put laudanum in her drink? What makes you think it was me?"

"Because you hate her; because you fetched the drinks from the bar and handed them out."

"I think you're crazy. If I hated her enough I'd put arsenic in her drinks, not laudanum. There were plenty of others who could have done it."

"But only one who could have been sure that she got it."

"Maybe it wasn't intended for her. If there really was laudanum in the stuff."

There was nothing to be learned from her; Brent turned away, his glance sweeping the bar. Lu had picked up the drinks from a place where either Biff or Shotgun could have got to them. There was Red Conrad to consider also. And the bartender. And probably a dozen others who could have reached the drinks.

Both Shotgun and Biff were missing. He went out into the street and walked to the saloon where Biff had been playing poker. Biff was no longer sitting in the game. Brent asked one of the players, "Where's Williams?"

"Went home."

"How long ago?"

"Ten, fifteen minutes."

Brent went out again. These were Biff's men; if he wanted an alibi they could be depended on to furnish it. He walked to Biff's shack, found it silent and dark, and slipped up to an opened window to listen. He heard the deep regular breath of a sleeping man. Didn't mean a thing; it doesn't take more than five minutes for a healthy man to fall into sound slumber. And he could pretend to be asleep in nothing flat.

Brent turned his steps towards Shotgun's shack. There was a light in it and when he looked through the window he saw Cuthbert sitting at a table studying a solitaire layout. He was fully dressed even to his hat. Brent went around to the front, grasped the door handle and pressed the latch and the door opened. He stepped quickly inside, kicked it shut after him. Shotgun wheeled about in the chair, tensed, then saw that Brent had not drawn his gun and got slowly to his feet. "What the hell do you want?"

"I want to know where you went after you left the Palace."

"What's it to you where I went?"

"Plenty." He advanced slowly and Shotgun began backing away. If he had not been so angry he might have wondered at this; Shotgun was not the one to back away from any man. He drawled, "I reckon you'd better start talking."

Shotgun gave a quick glance about him and backed away two more steps. He was near the stove. He growled. "What the hell's wrong with you, feller? You the kind to jump a man when he ain't got but one arm?"

"If you were where I think you were I'd jump you if you hadn't any arms. Cuthbert, *where were you?*"

"I come straight home; I been here ever since."

"I think you're lying. I think you climbed to the roof beside the Palace and got through the window into Judy's room." He was still moving slowly towards Shotgun, stalking him. Once more Cuthbert took a backward step. He stumbled against the wood box and put out his hand as though to brace himself against the wall. The hand darted into a dark corner and came away with the sawed-off shotgun he always used. He tossed it up, caught it deftly at the small of the stock and Brent heard the click of the hammer.

He dived under the weapon, hitting Shotgun just above the knees. He heard the roar of the gun, felt the blast of the explosion; then Shotgun went sprawling over his back.

Brent heaved upward and threw Shotgun's body clear, then whirled like a cat and pounced upon him. He tore the shotgun from Cuthbert's hand and hurled it the length of the room, then snatched out the man's Colt and threw that after it. He got up, dragging Shotgun erect with him. Cuthbert was big and strong but he was handicapped by his splinted arm and Brent's fury lent him double strength. He pushed Shotgun and the man sat down on the bunk.

Brent stood over him, his fists clenched. "Now I want the truth."

Shotgun's eyes blazed their hate but there was a hint of fear in them. He evidently thought he was dealing with a crazy man. He said, "I told you where I was. Dammit, I told you the truth."

Either he was sincere or a mighty good actor, Brent did not know which. He stood glaring down at Shotgun for a moment, then expelled his breath and took a backward step. "All right. If you did it you've got away with it so far; but I tell you, Cuthbert, I'm going to find the man who got into Judy's room and when I do I'm going to shoot him in his tracks."

"So somebody got into her room," sneered Shotgun. "By Gawd, Tex, you act like you was in love with the girl."

Brent turned abruptly and walked out of the shack. He made a circuit of the town, checking the occupants of the saloons, looking particularly for Red Conrad. He finally went back to the Palace and got Bub Whittaker to show him where Conrad lived.

Red had a room in a boarding house and they found the front door unlocked and a lamp burning on a stand at the foot of the stairs. Conrad's room was on the second floor and the door stood open. They went in and Brent struck a match. Red was sprawled across the bed, snoring. He had removed his hat and coat and gunbelt and one boot. It was plain to be seen that he was really sleeping and probably had been for some time. They went out again and Brent tersely related what had happened.

Bub said, "A feller that'll try a trick like that oughta be scotched like a sidewinder."

The Palace was closed when they returned to it and they parted. Brent went to his cabin, rolled a smoke and lay down in the dark to think. He did not try to deceive himself any longer; he loved Judy Clane and loving her he had to get out of Destiny. There was only one way to do this, marry her and take her away. He would have to come back to Destiny and finish the business which had brought him here, and she would have to wait for him, take her chance of his returning to her. If he failed to come back she'd be no worse off than she was at the present time.

He awoke early, his mind still on Judy, realized that the girls would not be stirring until noon or after and drifted off to sleep again. He got up at ten, cooked and ate breakfast, then walked to the Palace and circled to the alley. There was no way a man could gain the roof of the adjoining building without something to stand on and there was nothing in sight upon which to stand. He circled around to the front.

The building was vacant, having previously served as a store until Hannigan had built the more imposing structure on the other side of the street. The door was unlocked and Brent went in. A box stood in the middle of the floor and above it was a trapdoor in the ceiling. Brent got onto the box, pushed aside the trap and pulled himself into a loft. Directly over his head was a scuttle opening on the roof; he raised it and crawled through.

The four windows on the second floor of the Palace were directly under his observation and through one of them he could see a girl standing at the washstand combing her hair. He let his gaze sweep the roof, saw nothing which would give him a clue to the intruder and descended through the opening, pulling the scuttle back into place. He got down into the store, replaced the trapdoor and went outside.

He knew that Lil and Judy would be going to the Chinese restaurant for dinner and hung around outside the restaurant until he saw them coming up the street. He went inside and found a place at the table they usually occupied and when they entered he beckoned them to join him. Lil said, "Hi-yuh, Tex," but she did not smile and she said it as though her heart was not in it.

They sat down and he had a chance to study Judy. Her face was pale and she held her lips tightly compressed. She said, "Lil told me about somebody getting into the room. It seems that I'm indebted to you again. They kept telling me that one drink of whiskey wouldn't hurt me and while I thought it tasted funny I drank it."

They did not speak again until they had been served, then Brent said, "I've been trying to find out who it was but I haven't had any luck yet."

"I'd like to get my hooks into him myself," said Lil. "The kid's all upset. A girl can take care of herself when she's conscious but she's just out of luck if she's doped. It's a damned shame."

"You have any idea who put the laudanum in your drink, Judy?"

She shook her head. "I wasn't watching; I just took the drinks Lu gave me."

"She was in on it, but the one I want is the fellow who was back of it."

Neither of them had anything to offer along this line but guesses, and they finished their meal in comparative silence. Brent walked back to the Palace with them and at the rear door he said, "I'd like to go upstairs and look around a bit."

They went up to the room and Brent nosed about scanning furniture and floor and finally stopped at the opened window. There was a small nail in the frame which had once served to hold a curtain in place and on it he found a few black threads. He showed them to Lil. "Where would you say these came from?"

Lil studied them. "Looks like black broadcloth."

"Could they have come from anything of yours or Judy's?" She shook her head. "Nothing that I can think of."

"Who wears a black broadcloth coat?"

"Uncle Jim Ferguson, Jack Roselle, Biff Williams, Faro Pete, most of the gamblers at the Palace and other joints. Red Conrad has one. A dozen others about town. Might not even be a coat; the feller mighta got his pants snagged when he was squeezin' through the window. Count all the black pants in Destiny and you'll run out of numbers."

He nodded grimly. "At least it's something to start on. Keep your eyes open for torn black broadcloth." He turned to Judy. "You've got to get out of Destiny. Pack your stuff and be ready to ride. We'll go to Juniper and be married and I'll leave you in a safe place until I've finished what I came to Destiny to do."

She regarded him intently for a moment then slowly shook her head. "No, Tex, I'm not going. I don't want it that way."

"Why not? Don't you see it's the only way?"

She shook her head again and he saw two bright spots of color in her cheeks. She said, "Don't think I'm not grateful to you for what you've done, Tex. I am. You've been swell and I'll never forget you; but I won't marry you just to get away from Destiny."

"But you can't stay here, you're not safe as long as fellows like Biff and Shotgun are around."

"I'll be all right now that I know what to look out for. I promise you I won't drink any more laudanum."

He begged her then, his love sweeping over him like a tide. He could not move her and finally her obstinacy silenced him. After all, he reminded himself, he was an outlaw, a man with a price on his head because of that train holdup, a target for the gun of every lawman. He said, "All right, Judy; if you want it that way, that's the way it'll be. Take care of yourself."

He turned and walked from the room and Lil followed him out. He halted at the head of the stairs and turned to find out what she wanted. Lil looked as though she were about to explode. "Of all the prize saps," she said softly, "you win the handsome crocheted bathtub! Tex, for the love of Pete, if you want a girl to marry you *tell her you love her*."

He was annoyed. "If I didn't love her why in hell would I ask her to marry me?"

"Because you pity her, of course. The other day you told her you wouldn't marry anybody, that you couldn't be bothered dodgin' handcuffs and rollin' pins at the same time, and now all of a sudden you say, 'You gotta get out of Destiny; put on your hat and I'll take you to Juniper and marry you.' What *could* she think?"

"Good gosh, Lil, I didn't mean it that way at all!"

"Maybe you didn't; but now you'll have a sweet time convincin' her of it."

He realized now that she was right. He had gone about the thing in the wrong way. He should have made love to her, showed her that he really cared before asking her to marry him; but he had been so concerned over her safety, so anxious to get her away from Destiny that he had spoken what was in his mind bluntly, taking it for granted that she would understand that he wouldn't ask any girl to marry him unless he really loved her. Now, as Lil had said, he would have a sweet time convincing her that he wanted to marry her for herself alone and not because he pitied her and could see no other way of extricating her from the whole sordid mess.

Angry with himself, he sulked in his shack the rest of the day and went to the Palace late in the evening. There was only one thing to do: start at scratch, court Judy as a girl expected to be courted. He looked for her at once and found her at a table with Biff Williams, and went to the bar to wait until Biff left.

Time passed and Biff did not leave the table. Tex remained at the bar, drinking sparingly, holding his impatience in check. Lil joined Biff and Judy and Williams said something to her and she went over to the piano, sat down and started to play a waltz. Biff got up and Judy got up with him and he took her into his arms and started dancing. He was big, but light on his feet and a graceful dancer. Brent left the bar and walked over to the edge of the dancing space. Other couples had gone on the floor and were shuffling about and now he thought he would have his chance to get Judy alone.

Lil finished the number and the couples returned to their tables and ordered drinks. Brent caught Judy's eyes on him and thought there was a frightened appeal in them. He stopped behind Biff's chair and spoke over his shoulder. "May I have the next dance, Miss Clane?"

Judy shifted her gaze to Biff and it was Biff who answered. "You may not, Mister Tex. Miss Clane's engaged for the evenin'."

"I reckon that's sort of up to Miss Clane, isn't it?"

"It is. How about it, Judy? Do you dance with him or don't you?"

Judy was looking steadily across the table at Biff. She didn't answer for the space of ten heartbeats, then she looked up at Tex, her gaze direct and level. "I'm sorry, Tex, but I've promised every dance to Biff. Some other evening maybe."

She did not smile and the fear was still in her eyes. He looked intently at her for a moment, trying to read what was beneath that look, then bowed stiffly and turned away. He went to the bar and ordered three double whiskeys in succession. She had turned him down cold, and for Biff.

Jack's toneless voice spoke to him. "Take it easy, Tex. Better go home and get some shuteye; we ride in the morning."

Again the word had been passed and again he had missed it. He swore in disgust and exasperation and strode from the room.

CHAPTER ELEVEN

BRENT awoke feeling miserable. It wasn't a hangover; there was an emptiness within him that ached. Had Judy wanted to dance with him all she had to do was say so; Biff wouldn't keep her from him, he'd have seen to that.

He ate a tasteless breakfast and walked to the livery corral to get his horse. He rode to the Palace and found the other boys waiting. Presently Jack came riding around the corner leading the packhorse; he looked them over with his cold eyes, tossed the lead rope to Stub Shelly and said, "This way."

They rode north and as they emerged at the end of the street Brent saw the camp the stranger, Lem Purdy, had pitched. Lem sat in front of a fire with a skillet in his hand; he waved to them, then became intent again upon his cooking.

Brent asked Jack, "Find out any more about him?"

"No. Pretty closemouthed. Wants to ride with us, but we'll let him stew a while longer."

They followed the same course they had taken before and camped where they had camped on the first night of the previous raid. The men were in good spirits, but Brent was silent and morose. Judy would be at the Palace laughing and drinking with Biff. He played poker mechanically and was glad when the game broke up and they turned in.

The lack of progress in his search irked him; he was no nearer to knowing who the unknown leader was than he had been at the start. He was still inclined to favor Jack Roselle. If only Lu would loosen up!

They changed direction the next day, heading more to the northwest, and Brent guessed that they were going to tackle a train on the main line. As they pressed on at a trail lope he was gradually seized with the feeling that they were being followed. There was nothing tangible; he saw no one when he scanned the back trail and he heard no sound of pursuit when they halted to rest their horses and stretch their legs. Because there was no evidence of a trailer he did not mention his hunch to Jack.

Towards the end of the afternoon they topped a ridge and saw a town sprawled below them and about five miles distant. The town was on the railroad for Brent saw the smoke from a passing train. Jack said to him, "That's it. Train carrying specie stops for water around midnight."

Jack turned off the trail, led them back into the hill to a hollow with a spring and pulled up. "We'll camp here. No fire. Stub, throw something together that we can eat cold. Tex and I will scout ahead."

He and Brent rode back to the main trail and followed it to town. The name of the place, Jack told him, was Mescal and it was a fairly large place. They rode boldly down the main street, drawing no more than an occasional indifferent glance. The station was at the far end of the street and they dismounted before a saloon and went inside for a drink. They came out and seated themselves on a watering trough and smoked. From their position they had a view of the right-of-way for several hundred yards in both directions.

Jack spoke softly. "That water tank a hundred yards west of the station is where the train will stop. Those trees about fifty yards back is as close as we can get with the horses. We'll leave them there with Stub and sneak down to the tank just before the train's due. We'll figure out our play then."

They rode back to the camp to find that the rest of the men had eaten; but food had been saved for them and they had a meal of bread, cold meat and peaches. There was no fire and when dusk fell they stretched out on their blankets and talked quietly. It was around ten when Jack gave the word to move.

They followed the trail to within a mile of Mescal, then swung off towards the west, circling for the trees Jack and Brent had seen. The uneasy sensation of being followed had left Brent but he felt depressed and apprehensive. He told himself it was because of Judy and tried to shake off the feeling.

When they reached the trees they dismounted and tied, then sat hunched on the ground. There was no smoking lest the flare of a match betray them. Jack said, "I can't look at my watch, so we'll have to move to the tank when we hear the train whistle for brakes."

He spoke slowly, in his unusual monotone. "Stub will stay with the horses. Keep them sorted out in your mind, Stub, so you can give each man his own when he sings out his name. If you get them mixed up and we have to get out in a hurry each man'll take the first one he gets his hands on and we'll switch after the getaway. Red, you'll take the engine crew; if they don't do as you say, wing 'em. Frisco, you and Hawley will take care of the train crew and the passengers. Tex and I will handle the express car. If the door is locked and the messenger won't open it we'll use a stick of dynamite. We'll carry the specie box to the horses. Got it?"

They said they had, but to make sure Jack made each man repeat the instructions he had given.

The minutes ticked by. Brent, oppressed with a strange premonition of danger, got up and circled the patch of woods, peering into the blackness, stopping often to listen. He saw or heard nothing to alarm him. Perhaps, he told himself, the feeling was generated by his dislike of the job. He had not been cut out for an outlaw; he wasn't in the business for the wealth or the thrill; he was in it because it offered him the only means of getting at the murderer of his father and his brother. He made up his mind that never under any circumstances would he shoot to kill those who were fighting on the side of the law; if he had to shoot he would try only to disable. When he rejoined the men Jack asked, "All clear?" and he answered, "All clear."

"She's comin'!" exclaimed Stub, and they all listened. They heard a faint humming rumble that grew steadily louder and they got to their feet and stood waiting. Then came the distant whistle for brakes and Jack said, "Let's go!"

Brent went to his horse and drew the rifle from his saddle. In the darkness they did not notice that he was carrying it. They moved in a body from the blackness of the trees and headed for the water tank which loomed against the starlit sky. Out in the open Brent felt naked, but there was no movement within range of their vision.

They reached the tank and Jack said, "Red, stay right here. The trail will stop with the engine opposite the tank. Get behind one of those timbers so the headlight won't pick you up and wait until the fireman gets up on the tender before you jump them. Hawley, you and Frisco come with Tex and me. We'll wait about where the express car will be."

The four left the shadow of the tank and walked along the path which paralleled the rails. Jack noticed the Winchester under Brent's arm and asked, "Why the rifle? This'll be close work."

"It'll come in handy if we have to run for it."

"Better leave it when we tackle the car. It'll be in your way." Jack told him.

A pinpoint of light ahead of them grew larger and they knew it for the engine headlight. They moved away from the tracks and Jack said, "Lie down flat and don't move until the engine passes."

They flattened themselves on the ground and the light grew in size until it was a giant eye looking for the tank ahead. The fan of light swept by them and Brent, looking up, saw the fireman standing on the tender. The train shuddered and came to a jolting stop, bucked ahead another few rods and stopped again. The blank side of the express car was directly opposite them.

They were all on their feet now, and Brent was crouching behind Jack, the rifle gripped firmly in his hands. He looked back along the train; there were four coaches following the baggage car and all were lighted but the last one. He said quietly, "Jack, take a look at that rear coach. It's dark."

Jack, who had been watching the engine and waiting for a signal from Red, glanced towards the rear of the train. He said, "Probably an empty," and turned his attention once more to the front. Brent continued to watch that rear coach. Frisco and Hawley had moved to the rear end of the express car and were

67

standing just out of the light which came through the coach windows. From the engine ahead of them came a soft call, "Okay, boys!" and Jack said, "Here we go, Tex."

Brent did not move forward when Jack did; why, he was never able to say. Frisco and Hawley had moved nearer the coach; Jack strode swiftly to the door of the express car, tried to roll it back and found it locked. He rapped on it with his gun barrel and called, "Inside there! Open up or we'll blow it open!"

There was no answer. Frisco and Hawley stood tensed, their eyes on the coaches. Jack's call might bring a conductor or a brakeman. It didn't. Brent stooped and sent a glance underneath the cars. He could detect movement on the far side of the train and there were shadows in the patches of light from the windows. He snapped erect, called sharply to Frisco and Hawley, "Watch it! The other side!" and even as he said it flame stabbed the darkness beyond the platform of the coach and the roar of a riot gun shattered the air.

The charge of buckshot caught Hawley squarely in the middle and almost blew him apart. He fell backwards and hit the earth with the inertness of a wet sack. Frisco thumbed his Colt, firing in the general direction of the platform and started backing away. Brent, glancing swiftly towards the darkened car, saw men coming from both front and rear in swift, shadowy streams.

He yelled, "Jack! We got to get out of here!" and started pumping his Winchester. He aimed low, splintering the ballast stone and sending the pieces into the faces of the approaching men. Frisco passed him, swearing, trying to reload his gun; Jack came up at a run, his Colt flaming. Another blast from the riot gun sent buckshot screaming through the air above them. Jack cursed as the hammer of his Colt fell on an empty.

Brent said, "Run for it; I'll hold them off." They ran for the trees and he dropped to a knee and levelled the rifle. He shot carefully, coolly, hoping that none of the bullets would kill. His targets were moving shadows but the steady fire pinned down the posse, sent them crawling beneath the coach to the safety of the far side.

When he had emptied his Winchester he drew his Colt and started backing towards the trees. He fired steadily, sending the slugs into the side of the dark coach. He caught sight of a man running from the direction of the engine and when guns started blasting from the cab he knew it was Red Conrad. He saw Red stumble, recover and keep running.

Jack shouted from the trees, "This way, Tex! Hurry it up!"

Brent's gun was empty and there was no time to reload. He sprinted for the woods.

The firing behind him broke out anew as men started chasing him. Lead whistled overhead and kicked up dust all about him. There came a sharp blow on his right heel and his foot went numb for a second; he stumbled into the deep darkness of the trees, saw a horse and snatched at the bit. He swung into the saddle and got out of there fast, following the crashing ahead of him which told of the flight of his companions.

They reached the far side of the woods and Brent saw that there were four of them in the saddle; and then his eyes, sweeping the level stretch between them and the town, found a dark, swiftly moving mass and knew it for a body of horsemen. They were angling to head the outlaws off. He yelled, "Jack! Turn right! Turn right!"

They swung away and the posse swung with them. It was ride now or die and they rode. They rode blindly at first, letting their horses find the best way, and they followed the general direction of the railroad over level ground. And because they rode good horses that had been kept in condition they gradually drew away from their pursuers. At the first opportunity Jack swung towards the south and headed for the hills.

They rode all night and when daylight came they split into two parties, dividing the trail to confuse their pursuers. Jack and Brent rode together and spent hours hiding their trail. Stub Shelly and Frisco had also been instructed to cover their tracks and make for Destiny only when they were sure they were no longer being followed.

Late that afternoon after having been in the saddle continuously for seventeen hours, Brent and Jack found a mountain park with grass and water and got stiffly from their jaded mounts. They off-saddled, staked out the animals and dropped in their tracks. They had left the packhorse and were without supplies. They were too tired to care; they rolled in their blankets and slept.

They resumed their journey around three in the morning and now, refreshed and feeling comparatively safe, they talked things over. Hawley was dead, Red Conrad was missing and probably wounded, Frisco had a flesh wound in his side. Brent's bootheel had been shot off and there was a hole in his coat sleeve and another in his hat but he was uninjured. A bullet had scratched Jack's neck and he had bound his scarf over the wound to stop the bleeding.

Brent said, "They were laying for us. There was a posse riding that rear coach and another one in town all mounted and ready to go. I had a hunch that we were riding into trouble but it was so crazy that I didn't mention it to you."

Jack said, "Well, you saved the bacon again. You sure are a good one to take along. It was the rifle that held them off."

"I'm wondering who tipped them off. Somebody did. You reckon that stranger, Lem Purdy, followed us and managed to get word ahead?"

"Sure looks like it. We'll find out when we get back to Destiny. Nobody knew where we were headed but me and—" He broke off abruptly.

"Yeah?" prompted Brent.

"Nobody but me and you boys," said Jack in his toneless voice. "And you didn't know it until we were on the spot."

It wasn't what he had started to say, Brent was sure. He had been about to name another. It began to look as though Jack was not the man Brent sought after all.

CHAPTER TWELVE

THEY rode into Destiny shortly after dark and went directly to the restaurant. They ate until they could hold no more, then Jack rode to the Palace and Brent took his horse to the livery corral.

The Palace was going full blast when he entered the place, and a quick glance told him that Frisco Pete and Stub Shelly had not yet returned. Jack had changed his clothes and was standing at the end of the bar; Biff Williams was at a table with Judy and Shotgun Cuthbert hung around in the immediate vicinity. Brent saw that Shotgun had discarded the sling and was supporting the injured arm by thrusting it into his buttoned coat. The Cockeyed Kid was at the bar and the stranger, Lem Purdy, was apparently asleep in a chair by the wall.

Brent stared intently at Judy but she did not appear to have seen him. She was talking with Biff and sight of them together brought a feeling of emptiness to him. He went over to Jack and asked, "Learn anything about Purdy?"

"He was in town the whole time. Hannigan said he came into the store around noon of the day we left and bought a lot of supplies, and he was here at the Palace both nights. Looks like our hunch was wrong."

"Somebody passed the word; both of those posses were laying for us."

"I know. I'm looking into the movements of every man in town. If I find out who it was I'll shoot him myself."

Brent nodded. "Like the fellow they found in the alley, huh? He was a lawman, wasn't he?"

"Slim Cole? I don't know. I didn't kill him."

Brent's hunch that Jack was the leader was fading fast. He walked over to the bar and took a place beside Bub Whittaker. Bub asked, "How'd you make out?"

"Bad. There was a posse riding the train and another one waiting in the town. Notice anybody missing while we were gone?"

The Cockeyed Kid thought it over, then shook his head. "None that I can recollect. That there stranger was here every night."

"Jack tells me he bought a lot of grub; guess he's staying."

"The boys'll make sure of him before they take him on." The crossed eyes turned to Brent. "You know, Tex, if the law ever starts filterin' into Destiny there's gonna be one hell of a cleanup. Boys are gittin' careless; they been playin' in luck so long they're crowdin' it."

Brent thought things over while he drank. He didn't like the situation. Somebody had tipped off the law to the raid, but nobody was supposed to have known of it in advance except Jack and one other. He began to believe that the hunch he had that they were being followed wasn't so crazy after all. But who could have followed them, guessed their destination, then slipped around them to give a warning signal?

He found an answer to that. If this Purdy had a fellow camping in the nearby hills he could have passed the word that Jack's gang was riding and put him on the trail. The fact that Purdy had brought such a quantity of supplies lent weight to this theory, for Purdy would naturally do the buying for his companion rather than have him be seen in Destiny.

Brent didn't give a hoot for the safety of the outlaws; he had no sympathy for them, had become one of them only by force of circumstance. He'd have to look out for himself but to hell with the rest of the bunch. The only thing that worried him was that he might not find his man before the law closed in for the kill.

He became aware of somebody staring intently at him in the mirror and saw that it was Cliff Durham. The persistence of the man annoyed him; anybody else would have forgotten that tap on the skull long ago. An idea struck him. Durham was just a town marshal paid by the merchants to preserve the peace but he might be out to make a name for himself. He said to the Cockeyed Kid, "See you some more," strolled around the room watching the play and finally wound up beside Jack Roselle. He asked Jack in a low voice, "How's Cliff Durham for a suspect?"

"He was here the whole time," Jack told him, and that settled that.

Brent lounged at the bar watching Judy. Biff Williams made a final remark, leaned over and kissed her on a quickly turned cheek, got up and walked away. Instantly Shotgun Cuthbert shuffled forward and dropped into the chair Biff had vacated. Brent heard him say, "Evenin', sweetheart; how about another drink?"

The face she turned to him was cold, impersonal. "Nothing but double whiskeys tonight."

"Okay, okay." Shotgun called to a bartender, "Two doubles."

Jack said to Brent, "She's piling up commissions fast. Nothing but doubles and she's drinking tea."

Judy did not glance at Brent and the old yearning for her filled him. She talked with Shotgun but she did not smile. Shotgun tossed off his whiskey then leaned over the table and spoke to her in a voice so low that Brent could not hear what he said. She listened absently, her gaze on the far side of the room. Shotgun raised his voice, "Hell, you ain't even listenin' to me."

She looked at him then, let her gaze fall to his empty glass. "If you want to sit here you'll have to keep on buying."

"Not for no clam like you. I'll wait until you're feelin' better." He got up and slouched away, scowling at Brent as he passed.

Jack said in his monotone, "That jasper wearies me; some day I'm going to take him apart."

"You'd better make it soon," said Brent, "or I'll beat you to it."

He glanced over at Lu Roselle's table and found the green eyes fastened on him. She crooked a finger and beckoned to him.

"Lu didn't like my telling her to lay off the Judy girl," said Jack. She's probably going to give you merry hell. Go on over and get it."

Brent said to a barman, "Two for Lu's table," and went over and sat down. He forced a grin, raising the corner of his mouth and lifting an eyebrow. "Jack told me to come over and collect

72

a little hell. Lay it on thick, honey; I'd like to see him laugh just once."

The green eyes were smouldering. "Why did you get him to tell me to lay off that Judy girl?"

"Because you had her so scared she couldn't do her work. Now look at her; she's doing more business than all the rest of the girls together."

She waited until the bartender had brought their drinks, then said, "It's a wonder you're not hanging around her table."

"Maybe I don't like buying double whiskeys."

"Biff Williams seems to enjoy it; he's been hanging around her ever since you left."

"Maybe he's in love with her." He tried to keep the bitterness out of his voice.

"How about you?"

"I told you there's nothing between Judy and me. She even turned me down when I asked her for a dance."

The green eyes lost some of their fire as she looked across the room at Judy. One of Biff's men had taken Shotgun's place and was buying double shots. Judy hadn't even glanced towards their table. Lu looked back at Brent and smiled faintly. "Okay, darling." She caught a bartender's eye and raised two fingers. "These are on you, but they're singles."

After a while Brent got up and walked away. He had wormed himself back into Lu's good graces and might learn something from her yet. He strolled around the gambling layouts, losing a bet here and there, his glance going often to Judy's table. The man she was with was tall and goodlooking; he kept buying drinks and presently Judy was smiling at him and letting him hold her hand. Brent got madder by the minute.

When the time came for her act she leaned over, kissed the fellow lightly on the cheek and jumped up on the stage. She sang the songs they liked and when she had done her last encore jumped from the stage into the arms of the goodlooking outlaw. He kissed her and, holding her cradled in his arms, strode to the bar and called for drinks. She had not so much as glanced towards Brent.

He swore under his breath and walked over to the bar; he hadn't looked where he was going and found himself beside Shotgun Cuthbert. As he raised his glass Shotgun jostled him and he spilled some of the liquor. He set the glass on the counter. Shotgun said, "Pardon me!" and he said it as though he didn't mean it, which he undoubtedly didn't.

Brent took out a handkerchief and carefully wiped the liquor from his coat. He said in his drawling voice, "How's the arm coming, Shotgun?"

"Pretty good; just wearin' a wrist splint now."

"It's your left arm; it should bother your shooting any."

"Slows me up. When I can take it outa my coat I'll be all right."

"Hurry it up, will you? I'm getting sort of tired seeing you around."

"I'll be around long after you're gone."

Brent decided that he wouldn't enjoy getting drunk and moved about the place looking for trouble. Biff Williams had gone out and so had Cliff and nobody else gave him an excuse to pick on them. Judy and her goodlooking outlaw were still at the bar, drinking and laughing, and Brent finally went out and prowled about the town. When he returned to the Palace the goodlooking outlaw had gone and Judy was at a table with Shotgun. The sight did not help his temper any; he went over to where they sat and stood glaring at Cuthbert until he looked up. Brent said, "Get out; I want to talk with Judy."

Shotgun pushed back his chair and got up. "By Gawd, Tex, you can't order me around thataway!"

"Get out, I said."

Shotgun's face was flaming. "If it wasn't for this bum arm—!"

"Your gun arm's all right," Brent told him hopefully.

"You're damned tootin' it is!" Shotgun had raised his voice and those within reach of it were staring. "You'll find that out tomorrow. I'm warnin' you now to get out of Destiny by dark or you'll find out how good it is."

"That's too long to wait," drawled Brent. "Let's make it noon."

"That's just peachy! I'll git rid of this splint tomorrow and I'll be ready for you and rarin' to go." He backed away three steps, gave a curt nod and turned away. He shuffled the length of the room and went through the doors to the street.

"Tex!" It was Judy's voice, sharp, strained. He turned slowly and looked at her. The mask was gone and there was only fear on her face. She said, "He'll kill you!"

"Maybe." He sat down, leaned over the table. "Judy, I asked you to marry me and you turned me down. I thought afterwards that I'd gone about it wrong, but now I don't know. I believe now that this life has got into your blood, that it comes easy to make up to anybody who'll shell out the price of a double shot, including scum like Shotgun Cuthbert."

She winced as though he had struck her. "Tex!"

He went on, his voice tight. "The other night you wouldn't

even give me a dance. You had saved them all for Biff Williams. Tonight I learn that while I was gone you were entertaining Biff and liking it. Just how far that entertainment has gone I don't know, but I suppose that's your business."

The brown eyes were angry and there were spots of color in her cheeks. "It certainly is my business!"

He pushed back the chair and got up. "Okay, Judy, I won't bother you any more. I tried to help you, to make the tough spots a little easier for you, but you're learned the game fast. You don't need me any more. I was even fool enough to fall in love with you; but I'm not so foolish as to think that makes any difference to you."

He turned away, ignoring her agonized "Tex!" and walked blindly back to the bar. Lil slipped in beside him. She said in a low, angry voice, "What have you done to the kid now?"

He glanced at her, said, "Hello, Lil; have a drink."

"I don't want a drink. I want to know what you've done to Judy."

"Just told her what I thought of the way she's acting. I guess she didn't like it."

"Tex, honest to God you make me boil! Why don't you show her that you're in love with her instead of doin' your best to make her mad?"

"What good would it do? She doesn't love me. Why should she? I'm no prize beauty, I'm rough and tough and I'm an outlaw. She wouldn't even have security; I'd be like an anchor around her neck. Come on, have a drink."

"I told you I don't want a drink. Tex, you're the biggest damned fool in Destiny." She turned and flounced away.

Brent roved about the place, uneasy and miserable. It was nearing closing time and he would have gone home if he hadn't known that, tired as he was, he wouldn't sleep. Half an hour passed and then Shotgun came back in. He entered swaggering and he went directly to the table where Judy sat. She looked up at him, distaste written on her face. Brent started walking towards them without being conscious of it. He heard Shotgun say, "Feelin' better?"

Judy looked him over, her eyes passing over the reddish stubble on his cheeks and chin, down the dirty, wrinkled clothes and scuffed boots, then back again. She said, "No, I don't feel any better. I don't want you here, Shotgun; I just don't like you."

Anger flamed in his face. "Oh, you don't! And who the hell are you to play lady with me! 'Only double shots,' says you, 'and then I don't drink with Shotgun Cuthbert.' The hell you don't! You're gonna drink with me and you're gonna do the drinkin' at the bar and not at no private table."

He seized her by a wrist and jerked violently and she was pulled out of her chair. She cried out with the pain and seized him by the injured arm. He jerked away, but she had felt the object he held in the hand which was hidden beneath his coat.

Brent, a dozen feet away, said, "Turn her loose, Cuthbert!"

Shotgun let go her wrist, pushed her and she stumbled back into the chair. He turned slightly so that his right side was towards Brent, an awkward stance for a gunman. He grated, "Not tomorrow night and not tomorrow noon—now! Yank your iron and start shootin'!" His right hand fell to the butt of the Colt at his hip.

"Tex! The other hand! Look out!"

The blood was pounding through Brent's veins and Judy's voice seemed to reach him from a distance. The import of her words struck him like a sledge, explaining in a flash Shotgun's confidence, belligerence and odd stance.

He hurled himself to the left even as Shotgun's coat spewed flame and smoke; he felt the bullet from the small gun Shotgun held concealed in his other hand rake along his side. His own gun came out while he was falling and he fired instinctively and from the hip. If ever he had wanted to kill a man it was now.

He went crashing into a table and sent it skidding and heard Lil's startled yell as she fell out of her chair. He landed on his side, his gun still levelled, the hammer drawn back under a taut thumb. There was no need for a second shot; where once had glared a reddish eye in Shotgun's head was now a gaping hole. He stood there like a rock for the space of five heartbeats as though the huge body would defy death itself; then he plunged downwards, crushing a chair beneath him.

There was a dead silence; a silence that was broken by Jack Roselle's toneless voice. "Nice work, Tex. Belly up, everybody; the drinks are on the house."

CHAPTER THIRTEEN

BRENT got up slowly, his gaze still on the prostrate figure. Everyone in the Palace remained rooted, Jack's invitation for the moment ignored. In the frozen silence Lil's voice seemed inordinately loud. "For Pete's sake somebody help me up; I'm numb from the waist down."

It broke the spell; several men ran to her and hoisted her to her feet and she limped about holding her hip. Brent slowly holstered his gun, expelled the breath he had been unconsciously holding. He turned to look at Judy; she was on her feet supporting her weight on arms braced against the table. There was stark fear in her eyes. She cried, "Tex, you're hurt!"

He lifted the corner of his mouth in a mirthless grin. He touched the torn cloth of his coat, explored with searching fingers. They came away wet and red. "Nothing that a little courtplaster won't fix."

He glanced about him and became aware for the first time that two of Shotgun's men were watching him and that Jack was watching them. Jack had a hand inside his coat and had stepped away from the bar. They must have seen him for they made no move. Jack said, "It was a personal matter between Tex and Shotgun and it's been settled. I said drinks are on the house."

They moved in a body then, congregating at the bar. Men began talking and one of the girls laughed nervously. Brent caught a glimpse of Biff's profile; he was staring across the bar and his jaw muscles were tight.

Through the front entrance came Cliff Durham. He strode down the room on the far side of the game layouts, a hand on the butt of his Colt. His yellow moustache bristled and the pale blue eyes were glinting. He said, "What was the shootin' about?"

Brent faced him, tense and alert, although if it came to a shootout Cliff had all the advantage. Cliff's eyes were stabbing about, the body on the floor being out of the range of his vision. When nobody answered he moved slowly along the aisle, stopped abruptly when he caught sight of Shotgun's boots, then went over and stared down at the dead man. He wheeled to face Brent. "You?"

Brent had taken advantage of his distraction to put his hand on his holstered Colt. He nodded. "Yes."

Jack said, "Take a look at that splint of Shotgun's, Cliff."

Durham looked once more at the dead man. It was not necessary to examine the wrist splint; through the irregular blackened hole in the coat, just beneath the outflung right arm, he could see the muzzle of the short-barrelled gun which projected from the end of the bandage about Shotgun's hand. The whole story was written there to be read. Cliff looked at Jack and said, "Let's hear about it."

"Nothing to it. Shotgun got rough with one of the girls and Brent called him. If he hadn't, I would have. Shotgun told him to go for his gun and made a bluff at pulling his own; instead he cut loose with the hideout gun. Tex got wise in time and ducked—and scored a bullseye on Shotgun."

Cliff's gaze went slowly over the faces turned towards him then removed his hand from his gun and straightened. "Reckon that ends it," he said, and looked at Brent. The look said that he was sorry he couldn't make anything out of it.

Jack said, "The drinks are on the house, Cliff."

Brent moved to the bar and Cliff followed him. He said in a low voice, "I aim to get you yet, Tex; your luck can't hold forever."

"Don't go bustin' your arm just to use a splint, Cliff; I'm wise to that one."

"I don't need no splint; I don't need nothin' but old Betsy here." He tapped the gun at his side, downed his drink and moved away.

Judy had not come to the bar; she had dropped into a chair and sat with her elbows on the table and her face in her hands. She got up suddenly, walked in a wide circle about the body and went through the side door. Brent guessed that she wasn't used to seeing shot-up men.

Jack said, "Lil, run upstairs and fetch a blanket."

"Run? Are you kiddin'? I couldn't run if the place were afire."

"All right, walk then."

Lil went out the side door and Jack walked to where Shotgun lay, hunkered down beside the body and callously went through the pockets. He put the contents on the floor beside him, a half-filled sack of tobacco, papers, matches, pocket knife, the stub of a pencil, a buckskin purse. He opened the latter and dumped the money on the floor. There was a gold piece in it, together with some silver. He spoke to Brent. "You got first claim to this; want it?"

"Put it in the till and let the boys drink it up."

Lil came downstairs with a blanket and Jack said to a couple of his men, "Wrap him up in it and get him out of here. Tote him down to the jail; Cliff can see that he's planted." His gaze went over the men at the bar and fell on Bub Whittaker. "Cockeye, get a pail and a mop and do some swamping."

The body was removed, the floor washed and the life of the Palace once more flowed in its normal channel. The death of an outlaw was soon forgotten in this hardbitten community. Dice rattled, the ivory ball clicked, there was the clink of glassware and the ring of coins. Judy came in, a bit white of face, and took a place at a table as far removed from the spot where Shotgun had fallen as she could get.

Jack said to Brent, "Get Lil to go upstairs with you and patch up that side of yours. She's pretty good at it."

The wound was beginning to sting now and it was still bleeding. Brent beckoned Lil over, told him what she was to do, and they went up to her room. He stretched out on the bed and pulled the torn coat and shirt out of the way. The bullet had passed between thigh and lower rib, gouging out a chunk of flesh.

Lil got a bowl of water, poured some antiseptic into it and found some clean muslin which she tore into strips. She examined the wound with a practiced eye, said, "Good clean wound," and went deftly to work. She washed the torn flesh, put some kind of an ointment on it and bound it up. She said, "I reckon you know that if it hadn't been for Judy it'd been you they carried out in that blanket. She musta felt the gun when she grabbed his arm."

"Yeah, I know," he said glumly. "Why did she do it?"

"What do you think?"

"I think it was a damfool question; she did it to pay me back for what I did for her."

"You're still the biggest jackass in Destiny," she told him shortly.

"I'm wrong," he said bitterly. "She did it because she's crazy about me. That's also why she hangs around with Biff Williams so much."

Lil gave him a shrewd look. "Maybe you're nearer right than you think, big boy. Think that one over."

He stared at her for a moment, trying to comprehend; then shrugged it aside, thanked her for the neat job and went downstairs. The first thing he noticed was that Jack was not at the end of the bar; neither was he anywhere else in the Palace. He looked next for Biff and failed to find him. He went to Lu's table and asked her, "Where's Jack?"

"Gone outside to get some air. Sit down and have a drink."

He guessed the invitation was extended to keep him in the Palace, but it was one he could not very well refuse. He signaled a bartender and slid gingerly into a chair beside her. She said, "Still playing Sir Galahad I see."

"Nope. Just hunting down skunks for myself. I told you I hated Shotgun."

"Giving her up to Biff without a struggle?"

"Judy? I never had her to give up. If she wants Biff, that's her business."

She gave him a long look, the green eyes half veiled. "There are others. Some of them have red hair. Tex, I'm getting pretty fed up with this joint, I'd like a change."

He returned the look. "I could do a lot worse, honey. I'll take it up with the Board of Directors. Right now I'm going home and get some clothes on that are less ventilated and sticky. See you later." He got up and walked casually down the aisle and through the front doorway.

He made a circuit of the town, looking into saloons and stores for Jack and Biff and did not find either. Their absence at the same time could mean that one of them was the big boss or it could mean that neither was and that they had gone to consult with the one who was over the death of Shotgun.

He made his way to Biff's shack and found it dark and silent. Jack Roselle's house was equally deserted in appearance. Giving up the search, he made his way to Shotgun's cabin, found the door unlocked, and entered. He barred the door, hung a blanket over the one window and lighted a lamp. He searched the place thoroughly, hoping to find a clue to the identity of the unknown leader. He found nothing of that sort at all.

He turned his attention to hidden loot, tearing the place apart in his search. He was rewarded when he raised a cracker-box cupboard which hung from the wall on leather straps. Beneath it he traced out the outline of a rectangular section in one of the logs; removing this he found a recess in the log. In the recess was a cigar box and in the cigar box gold and silver coins, mostly gold. He guessed there was around five thousand dollars, Shotgun's share of stagecoach loot.

He found nothing more. The floor was of hard packed earth and there was no trace of spade work; there were no more recesses in walls or overhead beams. Brent took the box, blew out the light, investigated through the dark window and partly opened door, then glided away into the shadow. He thought swiftly, then walked by way of the alley to the back of Jack Roselle's house. He went into the stable, mounted the side of a stall and put the box on top of a rafter. It would not be spotted here even in the daylight.

He walked towards his shack and when still some distance from it crossed the street and moved silently through the shadows, eyes stabbing at the darkness. Shotgun undoubtedly had friends; Brent remembered the two whom Jack had kept under observation and thought it quite possible they might try to ambush him.

Across from the shack he halted and leaned against the wall of a cabin watching and listening, and presently he made out a bulky shadow a bit blacker than the tree by which it stood. When the shadow moved he knew it for a man. He eased out into the street, stealing gradually closer to the watcher. The man was intent on the far side of the street and was entirely unaware of his approach. Brent drew his gun, levelled it and said softly, "Hold it, you!"

The dark bulk did not move for an instant, then two hands slowly came up until he could see them above the man's head. The man said, "That you, Tex?" His voice told Brent that he was Cliff Durham.

"You, huh? Waiting for me, Cliff?"

There was a short pause, then, "Call it watchin' out for you. Couple of Shotgun's friends left the Palace and I figgered they might have idears."

"You're mighty kindhearted all of a sudden," drawled Tex. "Sure you weren't afraid they'd beat you to it?"

"If you want to put it thataway it suits me."

"Suppose you go ahead of me into the shack, light a lamp and take a look around, huh?"

Cliff lowered his hands and stepped out into the starlight, Brent close behind him. He didn't trust the marshal any farther than he could toss a brindle steer by the tail. When Cliff went into the shack, Brent stepped to one side of the doorway and waited until Durham had lighted a lamp, then entered and said, "Have a chair. You can protect me while I change my clothes."

He got undershirt and shirt, carrying his Colt around with him and keeping one eye on the marshal. It occurred to him that if Cliff really wanted to get rid of him he could plunk a bullet into him and pretend it had been done by one of Shotgun's friends. Perhaps it would be best to have the thing over with here and now.

Brent put his gun on a table in a corner of the room. Cliff, he had heard, was mighty fast on the draw but he would have to be lightning itself to get his gun out before Brent could snatch up his own. Brent shed his coat and shirt carefully, disengaging one arm at a time and keeping his gaze fixed on Cliff. There was a brief moment when each garment was before his eyes and at those times Cliff would have his chance to get to his feet and draw. Evidently the marshal did not think the risk worth taking; he watched Brent keenly but made no move and when Brent was finally dressed he said, "Figger you're able to do your own protectin' now?"

Brent said he guessed he'd managed and Cliff got up and went through the doorway to the street. Brent followed him but left the lamp burning. Durham moved quickly along the street and Brent, after watching him for a moment, went in the opposite direction. He holstered his Colt but kept his hand near the butt. He knew that he dared not relax his caution for a single instant.

He reached the Palace without meeting a person and entered it just as Judy began her act. The customers crowded up to the stage and Brent walked towards the end of the bar, noticing as he did so that Jack Roselle had returned. He took a place beside Jack, turning his back and hooking a heel on the rail. Judy was still shaken by the shock of the conflict between Shotgun and Brent, but she did a pretty good job of singing.

Jack said in a low voice and quite unexpectedly, "How'd you like to take over Shotgun's gang?"

Brent experienced a thrill which travelled the length of his spine and set his toes to tingling. It had come! He said as calmly as he could, "Me? I'd like it fine. Question is how are Shotgun's men going to like it."

"Don't worry about them. You're twice the leader he was and they'll soon find it out. Ever try your hand at holding up a stage?"

"No; but then I'd never tried my hand at holding up a train either."

"For a beginner I'd say you did pretty well. Hate to lose you from my bunch but you're too good a man to play second fiddle."

"How's Biff going to take it?"

"What's Biff got to do with it?"

"I figured the three outfits have some sort of working arrangement or they'd get in each other's way."

"You're a good guesser. Don't worry about Biff; he'll keep clear of you if you keep clear of him. Now go home and pretend to go to bed. After the Palace closes come around to my house. Back door. Go in and wait in the kitchen. Don't make a light."

Brent's blood was thumping in his temples. He had made it; tonight he would learn the identity of the man who bossed the three gangs; tonight he would face the man he was convinced had killed his father and his brother.

He did not let his elation show; he looked carefully over the crowd in front of the stage and saw Shotgun's two friends there. There was also Cliff Durham to avoid, for he wanted no trouble until he had learned the identity of the unknown leader; after that it couldn't come fast enough to suit him.

He went out through the side door and then into the alley. The light still burned in his shack and he reconnoitered carefully before entering it. He put out the light, removed his hat and gunbelt, putting the latter where he could snatch out the Colt at a moment's notice. He stretched out on the bunk and forced calm into his veins and muscles. Tonight was the night.

CHAPTER FOURTEEN

HE HAD about two hours to wait before the Palace closed and he lay there thinking and planning. When at last he met this man, what then? He realized suddenly that the climax would not have been reached, that his mission could not be completed until he had proved to his satisfaction that this was really the man who had murdered Benjamin Hollister.

Once the identity of the man was established, he could do some checking. He could find out where that person was at the time of his father's death, ascertain if he had an alibi for the night Cole was murdered, learn whether he had recently acquired any large amount of cash or property. There was even the possibility that he would be given the man's real name. If that name was Shell or something like Shell he would be reasonably sure he had found his man. Once satisfied that he was right the rest would be easy; he would bluntly tell him why he had come to Destiny, kill him and get out of there. And because she would never be safe in this wicked town he'd take Judy with him if he had to sandbag her and tie her across the saddle.

The sound of light, quick footsteps outside the cabin rang the alarm bell in his brain and he snatched his gun and had it trained on the doorway when the latch clicked. In the rectangle of the entrance he saw a form which was not that of a man. He said softly, "Who is it?"

"It's me, darling," said Lu Roselle, and closed the door behind her.

He swung his legs from the bunk and sat up and he was annoyed. She felt her way through the darkness and sat down beside him. She said, "I told Jack I had a headache and was coming home early. I've done it before. We have over an hour."

He said shortly, "You're plumb wrong; you're going home right now."

"Please, Tex!" She put an arm about him and drew him to her. She kissed him and pressed her cheek against his. "Let me stay, I'm so fed up with that joint I could scream." She clung to him and the words came in a rush. "Take me away from it! Let's go together. I don't care where just so it's away from here. I'll do anything you want me to, but get me away from this stinking hole!"

"Lu, you're crazy. What about Jack?"

"To hell with Jack! I tell you I'm fed up with it! All I do is sit, night after night the same thing. I want to get away; I want to see and do things; I want to be loved by something besides a chunk of animated ice! Listen, dear; I can get my hands on a big chunk of cash. Take me away from here and it's yours. We can live in style—travel, do things!"

At last she was talking and he was quick to take advantage. "Maybe if you had asked me before tonight I'd have been more than willing; but tonight I'm to see the big boss about taking Shotgun's place."

"Don't do it! Get out of Destiny and take me with you. I'm scared, Tex; scared as hell!" She clutched him tightly. "Things are beginning to go wrong. Shotgun's last raid was tipped off and so was Jack's. Somewhere in Destiny is a traitor. Other jobs will go wrong and some day a posse is going to ride into Destiny and clean up."

"You've been drinking too much tea," he told her.

"It's so and you know it! Look at Alder, at Jackson's Hole, at a dozen other outlaw hideouts. They got careless just as they've got careless in Destiny and the law caught up with them. Three gangs operating out of the one stinking little town! Three separate trails leading back to Destiny!"

"This boss of ours seems to be a smart fellow; can't we do

84

pend on him to pull us out of here before the law strikes?"

"In this game it's every man for himself; he's probably sitting pretty with a getaway all planned. Only a very few know who he is and they won't tell."

Brent's nerves were tingling. "Naturally I'm curious about him. Do I know him?"

"Of course."

"Does he use his right name?"

"I don't know."

"I wondered. Somewhere I heard a name connected with the outlaws of Destiny. A name that sounded like—Shell."

She drew away from him and he could feel her intent gaze through the darkness. She said in a hushed voice, "Shell?"

"Something like that." He tried to sound indifferent. "I didn't pay much attention. Doesn't matter; I'll meet him tonight and maybe I'll find out then."

A subtle change came over her; he could sense it in the way she reacted. She stood up. She said, "I guess maybe you're right; I'd better go home."

And then somebody knocked on the door.

Lu gave a gasp, then froze into silence; Brent snatched up the gun he had returned to the chair and asked, "Who is it?"

The answer came in an even, toneless voice. "Jack Roselle. I came to tell Lu the party's over."

Brent heard her whisper, "Dear God!"

The latch clicked and the door flew open but nobody stood in the entrance. Jack remained at one side of it, protected by the wall. He said, "Come on out, Lu."

"Jack, we've just been talking." Her voice trembled.

"Come on out."

Brent said, "Don't get us wrong, Jack."

"Come—on—out!"

Brent saw her move slowly towards the doorway. She said again, "Honest to God, Jack, we weren't doing a thing but talking."

"Sure, sure. Just come out and go home."

Brent got up from the bunk and watched as Lu went out, cringing as far from Jack's side of the doorway as she could. He heard Jack say, "Go home; I'll talk with you later." She turned quickly and Brent heard the click of her heels on the planks as she ran up the street.

Brent said, "I'll make a light and we'll talk this over."

"Don't bother. I'm not coming in and I know you won't come out. I could give the word that would turn every gun in Destiny on you but I'm not going to do it. You saved my bacon twice and it was Lu chasing you and not you chasing her. Be

85

out of Destiny by morning. You'd better leave right now before I change my mind."

Brent said nothing. He heard the soft sound of footfalls and then there was silence. He said, "Jack!" but there was no answer. Jack Roselle had gone.

He settled back on the bunk with a large chunk of lead at the bottom of his stomach. Gone now was his chance of meeting the man he had wanted so much to meet. Damn Lu Roselle! How had Jack found out? The answer was not hard to find. Cliff Durham had followed her and had seen her come into his shack. She had said that Cliff wanted to get something on her and Cliff had seen his chance and had taken it. That it was Brent's shack she had entered made the prospect of Jack's wrath even more satisfying to him.

After a moment Brent sat up and rolled a smoke. The lead in his stomach dissolved in the acid of resolution. He had to leave Destiny but that didn't mean he was licked. He'd still find his man. He'd camp in the hills and get Bub Whittaker to keep him supplied with grub. He'd take the old man into his confidence; he had to. Maybe Bub would tip him off when a raid was to be made and he could watch for the gang when it returned and follow the leader to their secret headquarters.

And Judy? He clamped his jaws determinedly. He'd take her with him; somehow he'd get her out of Destiny.

He got up and reconnoitered from within the shack then ventured into the darkness. He went along an alley, passed the rear of the Palace, rounded the corner of the empty building with the trapdoor in its roof, slipped through the doorway. He got up on the roof. There were lights in all four rooms but so far as he could see they were empty. He settled down to wait.

The Palace closed at last and the girls came up to their rooms. He saw Lil and Judy enter theirs, saw Lil come to the washstand and turn up the lamp. He walked silently across the roof to its edge, leaned over and rapped on the pane. Lil could not recognize him but she came over and raised the sash. He said, "Move back; I'm coming in."

Lil said, "Good grief, Tex, what are you—a Peeping Tom?"

She moved away and he half leaped, half dived through the window. He said shortly, "Lock the door."

Judy was staring at him, her eyes wide. She turned swiftly and shot the bolt. He said, "Keep your voices down. Judy, I've got to get out of Destiny before morning or be the target for every gun in town." He walked over to her and took her into his arms. He kissed her, then said simply, "Judy, I love you. I can't go without you. I haven't a damned thing to offer you but a lonely camp somewhere in the hills and a sure dose of lead poisoning if they find us. I'm a skunk for asking you, but will you go with me?"

Never had he looked into a face so transfigured. Radiance came into it, the soft quick glow of utter faith and devotion. The brown eyes warmed, a delicate pink stole into the cheeks, the red lips curved in a smile of infinite tenderness. She said, "Yes, Tex, I'll go with you. Anywhere in the world."

She stood on tiptoes and he bent down and kissed her on the lips. Lil said, "Good gosh and the cows come home!" and sat down on the bed. At the end of ten heartbeats she said, "Break, kids. For Pete's sake, Tex, sit down and tell us what happened."

He told them; told them with Judy's hand in his and an arm about her slim waist. He told them everything, trusting Lil but knowing that it didn't matter now whether or not she betrayed him.

"Then you aren't really an outlaw!" cried Judy softly. "You made up to Lu just to learn things. Oh, Tex, I've wanted to tell you about Biff but I didn't dare. That night of the dance he told me that if I didn't cut you cold he'd pick a quarrel with you and kill you. I hated to do it, but for—for your sake—" She started to cry, softly.

He drew her to him. "Never mind, honey; that's all past now. Get ready to leave. I'll find a horse and saddle for you. When you get your stuff together put out the light as though you'd gone to bed. I'll be back and we can get away over the roof. Savvy?"

"Yes, Tex." She raised her lips and he kissed her and then got up. He leaped over to the roof and descended through the trapdoor to the first floor, then followed the alley to the livery corral. The night hostler was asleep in the office; he got his horse and saddled up by the light of a lantern that had been left burning, then looked over the horses he knew were for sale. He selected a gentle little mare, found a small saddle and cinched it on.

* * *

Jack Roselle entered the living room to find Lu pacing the floor. She had done some hard thinking and had her story ready. She said before he could speak, "Jack, I went to Brent's place on business, our business."

"Interesting," said Jack coldly. "Tell me about it."

"Listen. Don't Tex remind you of somebody we both knew?"

His brows drew together. "Don't make a riddle of it. Who does he remind you of?"

"Slim Cole. I noticed it at once and when he started asking

questions about Slim I was sure. He's a brother or a cousin or something."

"What of it?"

"Why was Slim killed?"

"I don't know."

"I don't either, but I can make a guess. Slim asked me once if I'd ever heard of a man named Shell. Right after that he was killed. Tonight Tex asked me the same question. Slim and Tex are both looking for a man named Shell."

Jack was staring at her now. "Shell, eh?" He started pacing the room. He said at last, "That name evidently meant something to somebody and he had Slim rubbed out. I think I know who that somebody is." He turned abruptly and went out and Lu sank into a chair with a sigh of relief. She had got away with it; she was safe. She felt suddenly limp and weak.

* * *

Brent finished saddling up, then tiptoed into the office and put enough money on the desk to pay for the horse and rig and went out without awakening the hostler. He was about to mount his horse when he heard the quick thud of boots and snapped short, his hand dropping to his Colt. The Cockeyed Kid came up at a run. He said, "I've been lookin' all over for you, Tex. What the hell happened? Jack's rounding up all the hands he can find and I heard him tell one of 'em there's a bounty of fifty bucks on your hide. You gotta get out of Destiny on the run."

"Thanks, Bub; that's just what I'm fixing to do."

"Anyway I can help? I got m' hardware buckled on and I'm rarin' to go." He patted the gun at his hip. It was a Peacemaker Colt with a walnut butt and the holster was black and slick with age.

Brent said, "There's no time to explain now, but I'm going to the Palace for Judy. She's going with me. If you really want to help you can hold the horses for me. Will you do it?"

"You're danged tootin' I will! Let's go."

The old fellow swung into the saddle and they set out for the alley which ran behind the Palace. As they rode along at a quiet walk they could hear the pound of boots on the plank sidewalk as men ran towards the livery corral. They had got away just in time.

They halted a couple hundred feet from the Palace and Brent slipped to the ground. "If anything starts," he said tersely, "tie the horses and get out of here."

He walked along the alley, rounded the vacant store and stood at the street corner watching. All around he could see vague forms moving. He took a chance, slipped around the corner and into the building, then made his way to the roof. Lil's window was open and he called softly, "Judy!"

"Yes, Tex!"

"Think you can climb over me to the roof?"

"I'm so happy I could fly over!"

Footsteps sounded in the passageway beneath and a voice said sharply, "Who's up there!"

Brent stood rigid, not answering, hoping the man would move on. He didn't; he raised his voice in a shout, "Hey, fellers! Over here at the Palace! He's on the roof next door!"

Brent ran towards the scuttle, swearing under his breath. He heard answering shouts and the pound of boots as men approached. He started to lower himself through the scuttle hole, but drew back as he heard footsteps below. Somebody yelled, "The trapdoor's open! Sock it to him if he shows!"

Brent started for Lil's window, then abruptly changed his course. Judy and Lil must be kept out of this at all costs. He ran to the back of the building, threw himself flat and wiggled over the eaves. He hung for a moment, then dropped.

A gun roared just as he released his hold and he felt the bite of the bullet on his cheek. He jerked out his gun while he was in midair, landed like a cat and whirled. He saw a dark bulk and fired and the bulk folded abruptly. Somewhere behind him another gun roared; he wheeled and fired and heard the man scramble for the safety of the corner.

He started running towards the waiting horses and his heart sank as a whole body of men rounded the far corner of the Palace. He was cut off. He fired into the mass; a man went down and another one staggered. His gun was empty and he crouched low to reload and their lead swept through the air above him. He had the dismal feeling that he was licked.

And then from farther down the alley came a bloodcurdling yell and the thunder of hoofs, and the advancing men stopped in their tracks and turned. The Cockeyed Kid and the two horses were coming at a gallop.

Right through the mob they tore, scattering men to right and left. Bub's gun was blasting and at every shot somebody fell or staggered away. With a cry of exultation, Brent got to his feet and started running on a course parallel with that of the horses. A man leaped at him from the corner of the building but Brent hit him like a charging bull and sent him flying. Then his horse was abreast of him and he snatched the horn with his left hand, jumped and let the momentum carry him into the saddle.

He thrust the empty Colt into its holster and seized the rein

Bub pressed into his hand. Lead was whining about them, but it was dark and they were moving swiftly. At the next passageway he wheeled his horse sharply to the left and Bub swung with him. They reached the street and turned right and pounded along the main street.

The houses dropped behind them one by one, and then they were on the open range and headed for the nearby hills.

CHAPTER FIFTEEN

THEY rode hard, Bub choosing the route. He knew the country well and as dawn was breaking he led the way into a mountain park where there was grass and water and a cluster of trees which would afford concealment. When they reached the latter the Cockeyed Kid said, "You keep outa sight; I'm goin' back and cover our tracks."

Brent said, "I reckon you've paid me back plenty for that ten bucks. I don't want you to get into this any further than you are; when you wipe out those tracks get back to town as soon as you can. It was too dark in that alley for anybody to recognize you."

The Cockeyed Kid glared in his general direction, his jaw outthrust. "I ain't near paid back what I owe you. You don't need to tell me how you got into this mess; I'm gonna help git you out. You'll need grub for one thing and I kin fetch it to you."

Brent put a hand on his shoulder. "Thanks, oldtimer. Hunker down; I'm going to tell you a story."

They squatted on their heels by their horses and Brent told him everything. The old man listened without interrupting and when Brent had finished he nodded vigorously. "I'm with you, son, every jump in the road. I ain't got no quarrel with most of the boys but them fellers that are runnin' the show would let me starve rather than take me along and give me a cut. Say I'm too old! Hell, I can still outdraw and outshoot any one in the crowd. I'm in; that's flat. Got any idear who this feller you're lookin' for is?"

"I'm still guessing. How about you?"

"Jack Roselle."

"That's what I thought at first but now I'm not so sure. He spoke as though it was somebody else; I was to meet him after the Palace closed last night and he was going to take me to him. How about Biff Williams?"

"Second choice, with Cliff Durham runnin' a close third."

"Cliff?" Brent was surprised.

"Why not? As marshal he can mosey around anywhere he wants and can talk to any of the leaders without arousin' suspicion."

Brent thought this over. It was a new idea and he rather liked it. He asked, "How long has he been in Destiny?"

"Off and on for a year or more. Took the marshal's job three, four months ago. The three gangs usta tangle a lot among themselves, and once two outfits tackled the same job at the same time and had a hell of a fight over how to split. Right after that Cliff was made marshal to sorta keep order. Come to think of it, it was around about then that the three gangs started doin' different kinds of jobs."

Brent's face was tight. "Three or four months ago, huh?"

"Nearer four than three, I reckon."

"Cliff Durham! Bub, you may have something there. If it was Cliff I can understand why he never found my brother's killer." He got up and paced about, thinking hard. He turned at last to the old man. "Bub, you mean it when you say you'll stick with me? Never mind, I know you do. I've got to get a hideout nearer Destiny. This is too far away to operate. The man behind this thing is the one I must locate and I've got to be on the spot to do it."

Bub thought for a moment. "They's a old broke-down stable back of my shanty. The roof is caved in but they's a loft where you could hole up all right. Some of the boys keep their hosses in it and you could put yours there without it bein' noticed. But it's risky as hell, Tex."

"It'll do." Brent took out some money and handed it to Bub. "Buy some grub and cache it in that loft, stuff that don't have to be cooked. Do it today. Then if the coast is clear hang something white where I can spot it. I'll sneak in and hole up there."

Bub got to his feet. "I'll do it. You want I should get word to Judy that you're safe?"

"If you can do it without getting caught. I think Lil's on the square but don't tell them any more than that I'm safe."

"Reckon I'll have to turn this hoss loose before I hit town."

"No, you can keep her. I left money on the livery corral

desk for the horse and rig, but the hostler was asleep and don't know who bought her. You can say you did."

Bub nodded his understanding and got into his saddle. He said, "What gits me is why Jack set his dogs on you right after he give you till mornin' to git outa town."

"I made a mistake. I took a chance and mentioned that name Shell to Lu. She tightened up right after that. She'd noticed the resemblance between Slim Cole and me, and maybe he asked her the same question. I think she told Jack about it to square herself with him. If that name meant anything to Jack he'd get wise to me right away."

"Sounds like sense to me," agreed Bub. "Well, we've fooled 'em so far and we've got to keep on foolin' 'em. If you see a white rag on that barn you'll know the coast is clear as far as I can see it. So long and take care of yourself."

He rode away into the dawn and vanished in the mist about the entrance to the park. Once beyond it, he dismounted and painstakingly erased with a branch from a tree the few faint tracks which they had made, then headed in a circuitous route for Destiny. Occasionally he heard distant sounds, the tramp of hoofs, the crashing of broken brush, the voices of searchers. When he was a safe distance away from the park, he trailed one of these bunches, fell in behind the riders and rode as one of the party. They were working slowly but surely towards the park where Brent was hiding.

Biff Williams was leading them and Bub finally spurred up beside him. He said, " 'Scuse me, Biff, but I figger we're wastin' time." Biff glared at him but he went on. "Now this here Tex feller, he don't know the country; I jest can't figger him gittin' this far in such a short time. I figger he'd hole up at the first likely place he come to, or keep goin' right on to Juniper."

"Jack's outfit is ridin' the Juniper trail."

"Then I'd say he got the best chance of ketchin' him. But you jest can't tell me the feller got this far by hisself."

"You forget he had somebody with him."

"He did? I didn't know that."

Biff told him, rather profanely, about the unknown rider who had broken up the party in the alley.

"Betcha it was that stranger, that Purdy feller!" said Bub.

"We checked on him right away. He was in his blankets."

"Well, it wouldn't be one of the boys. I betcha it was that Purdy feller and when he got Tex in the clear he circled back to his camp so's not to show up missin'. That'd leave this Tex feller on his own. Naw, sir; if he didn't head straight for Juniper he's hidin' nearer town."

Biff led them on for a while longer but his heart was no longer in it and finally he turned and started back. When they neared Destiny they slowed their pace and began searching methodically. Bub said to Biff, "I reckon you fellers can handle him if you flush him. Me, I'm gittin' too old for this kind of stuff; I'm goin' home."

He rode into Destiny shortly before noon to find the town practically deserted. Everybody and his brother were out combing the hills for Tex. Uncle Jim Ferguson was standing in the doorway to his office and called to him and Bub rode over. Ferguson asked, "Any news?"

"Nope. I figger he rode right on to Juniper."

"I hope so," said Uncle Jim. "I like that boy, Bub. Just between you and me I hope he gets away. What does Jack want him for?"

"You can search me," said Bub. "I jest got the word that Jack'd put a bounty on his hide and figgered I could use the cash."

They chatted for a few minutes longer, but Bub wasn't telling anybody anything, not even a friendly cuss like Uncle Jim, and finally he said, "So long, Uncle Jim," and rode on to the store. He went inside and made his purchases, putting them into a gunny sack. He rode to his shanty, a tumbledown affair but neat and clean on the inside, and put his horse in the dilapidated stable. He climbed a rickety ladder to the loft, taking the sack with him.

The loft was a storage space for odds and ends of all kinds. There were boxes and old tools and discarded harness, broken chairs, a washstand with its doors torn off, singletrees, a stained straw mattress, rusty picks and shovels, and some kegs. Bub carefully rearranged these to form a protected nook and buried the sack in a pile of rubbish. Through the broken roof light fell in shafts to the floor below, but the loft was in gloom. At its rear was a small window with a shutter that hung by one hinge. Just enough light filtered in to permit moving about without stumbling over things.

Satisfied that he had done everything possible to make the hiding place secure, Bub sat down by a window in his shack and watched until he saw Lil and Judy come out of the Palace and walk towards the restaurant. He waited until they had gone inside, then entered himself. Two other girls from the Palace were there, but he was the only man. He sat down at the counter and ordered a plate of bacon and beans and a cup of coffee. He gauged it nicely and finished just as Judy and Lil got up from their table. He waited for them to pass and the friendly Lil thumped him on the back and said, "Hi-yuh, Bub!"

He said, "Hi-yuh, Lil," and followed them out, talking as they walked. "Done a mite of huntin' with the rest of the boys but I ain't as spry as I once was and come on in ahead of 'em." He fell in between them and spoke in a low voice. "Don't be s'prized at what I'm goin' to say; keep right on walkin' and actin' natural." He paused a moment, then said, "Tex is safe."

Judy gave a little gasp and said in a whisper, "Oh, thank goodness!" then began talking brightly to Lil. When they reached his shanty, Bub said, "Be seein' you," and dropped out. He was tired and there was nothing more he could do at the moment; he went inside and stretched out on the bunk to catch up with his needed sleep.

He awoke around four and walked up to the Palace. The searchers were beginning to drift back to town, so he had a drink, sat down along the wall and absorbed the information they gave when they entered. Everything was to the good; they had found not a sign of Tex and the general opinion was that he had headed straight for Juniper.

Biff and his bunch came in around five and reported the same lack of success. They had a drink and Biff said, "Maybe we've missed a bet by ridin' hell-bent out of town. That Tex jigger is foxy; maybe he circled and come back to town. I figger we ought to comb the whole of Destiny before dark."

He went trooping out with them and Bub followed in their wake. Biff sent several men on horseback to watch at the other end of the street, and took the rest of them, some on horseback and some afoot, to the town limits. He disposed his force to best advantage and they made a thorough and methodical search, going into every house and building on both sides of the street. Bub's shanty and the brokendown stable were included, of course, and quite naturally no trace of the fugitive was found. When the search was finished, Biff dismissed the men and stated flatly, "It's a cinch he ain't in town. I'm bettin' he rode straight to Juniper and that we won't see any more of him."

Bub ate his supper and went back to the Palace. All the searchers were in by this time except the bunch which had taken the Juniper trail with Jack. If they went all the way to Juniper, they would not be back until the next evening.

Ferguson came over and sat down in the chair beside Bub. He said, "Well, it looks as though he got in the clear."

"Sure does," agreed Bub. "They got any idea who it was that helped him?"

Ferguson gave him a searching look. He said cautiously, "I was hoping you'd be able to tell me that."

Bub shook his head. "Only one I talked to about it was Biff and he didn't know. I sort of figgered it was that Purdy feller, but Biff said he was all present and accounted for when they checked on him." He glanced about him and spoke in a lowered voice. "Sure it wasn't you, Uncle Jim?"

"No, it wasn't me. The first I knew there was anything going on was when I heard the shooting."

Bub did not stay until the Palace closed because he did not know when Tex would try to sneak into town. He went home early and stuck a bit of white cloth on the loft window. He sat down to wait.

It was nearly dawn when Brent halted his horse in the brush a hundred yards behind Bub's stable. He had traveled cautiously, taking his time, although he was fairly certain that the search for him would not continue through the night. He waited, squatting on his heels and smoking, his horse standing beside him over trailing rein.

The sky began to lighten and a faint glow stole over the eastern hills. The drab shacks which lined the alley began to take form and his gaze settled on the barn with the broken roof. A bit of white hung limply from the loft window. He got up, took the rein and started walking towards it. He was in the open but he had no alternative. His eyes stabbed at the mist which hung over the town, looking for movement. He saw none. He moved to the rear of the building, saw a doorway in its back. Bub's cautious voice reached him. "It's okay, Tex! Fetch him in."

He led the horse into the stable and the old man took the rein. "Skip up that ladder and git behind the trash. I'll take care of the hoss."

Brent went up to the loft carrying his blanket roll, saw the straw mattress which Bub had spread on the floor. He took off his hat and gunbelt and stretched out. Within five minutes he was asleep.

CHAPTER SIXTEEN

A PERIOD of inactivity dragged by, the more irritating to Brent because of his close confinement. His hope of learning the identity of the mysterious big boss still lay in his knowledge that the gang leaders reported to him after each raid and might eventually lead Brent to him if only he could stick close enough to their trail.

The day after Brent established himself in the barn Jack Roselle and his bunch returned. They had gone clear to Juniper without overtaking the man called Tex or finding any sign that he had gone that way, and nobody had seen him there. Biff was still combing the hills, but the trail was now cold and there were a lot of hills. The efforts to find Tex fell from the boiling point to a simmer and from there to dead cold. It was the almost universal opinion that the fugitive had circled Juniper and had kept going.

Nobody knew just what had happened to make his death so important to Jack and they didn't waste much time in speculation. It was sufficient that there was a reward of fifty dollars offered for Tex's death; the general run of them concluded that Tex had been playing around with Lu and had managed to get caught at it.

The Cockeyed Kid was the source of Brent's information. He reported each day, usually after dark when he fetched Brent a hot meal prepared by himself. Judy, he told Brent, was keeping her chin up and sticking to tea; she tolerated Biff, who was tiring somewhat of buying double shots without getting any return on his investment and could no longer scare her with threats of what would happen to Brent if she wasn't nice to him. Uncle Jim Ferguson was on another gold-buying trip; Lem Purdy still hung around awaiting the chance to go on a raid; Shotgun's bunch was still without a leader.

Brent had plenty of time to meditate and the meditation, while producing some interesting possibilities, did nothing to change his plans. One of the conclusions he reached was disturbing; it was quite possible that he was on a false scent and had been from the start. The man who had murdered Benjamin Hollister might not be named Shell or anything like it and might never have seen Destiny. But it was certain that Cole had been murdered in Destiny and logic still told him that the one who had done it had learned that Cole was searching for a man named Shell.

One night, tiring of inactivity, Brent sent Bub to locate Cliff Durham and upon learning that the marshal was at the Palace quickly saddled up and rode into the hills. He circled Destiny and came out on the road to Juniper and, finding the tree in which he had concealed the black robe, retrieved it and made his way back to the barn with it. Wearing it impeded his actions and restricted his vision, but it offered one precious advantage. Seen without it, he was a dead duck; covered by it, nobody but Cliff Durham would shoot without first learning the identity of the wearer. To lessen the danger of entanglement in its folds, he cut it off so that it fell only to his knees.

The days dragged on into a week, and then ran over into another week. Even the most persistent searchers had given up the quest and Bub reported that some of the outlaws were grumbling about the inactivity, the excess of caution being displayed by their leaders. Brent found it possible to venture out for an hour or two after nightfall, sometimes going afoot and at others exercising his horse. On such occasions Bub kept a careful watch, agreeing to hang a lighted lantern in the barn in the event of danger. Brent wore the black robe coming and going.

One night Bub paid him a visit after the Palace had closed, climbing the ladder to the loft and whistling as a signal. He slithered over to where Brent lay on the straw mattress. "You awake?"

"Yes. What's up?"

"The highway bunch is fixin' to go on a raid, I think. Feller named Pug Dowd come in lookin' important and started perculatin' around among Shotgun's men. I figgered he was passin' the word, and later Uncle Jim—he jest got back from his gold-buyin' trip—told me Pug had been put in Shotgun's place. I'll keep my eye peeled tomorrer mornin'; if they ride it'll be early."

"Bub, that's great! No way of finding out how long they'll be gone, is there?"

"Nope. Nobody knows that but Pug and the feller he gits his orders from. But you can count on a day goin', a day for the holdup, and a day returnin'. More likely be two goin' and one comin' back. Three, four days in all."

"Judy all right?"

"As fine as she can be. I slipped close to her when nobody was around and told her you sent yore love and I thought she was gonna kiss me. Her face lit up like a Christmas tree and I got away from there fast. Later I was standin' at the bar and she drug Frisco Pete up to buy a drink and slipped in beside me. When she got the chance she whispered, "Tell him I'm waiting for him.""

"For gosh sakes be careful, Bub. If they figure you in on the play I'll never forgive myself."

"Don't worry none about me, son. I wisht I could do more. Lil, she's keepin' her eyes open for tears in black coats and pants. Ain't had no luck yet. Wal, I'll let you know in the mornin' if Pug and the boys ride."

Brent was up early and was eating his breakfast when Bub came up the ladder. "They're ridin'. Headed south. Six of 'em, includin' Pug Dowd."

Although the gang would not possibly be back before the following night, Brent left nothing to chance. He packed enough cold rations to last him two days and as soon as darkness fell he descended the ladder and saddled his horse while Bub went up to the Palace to check on Cliff Durham.

Bub returned presently to report Cliff at the Palace and Brent headed out across the open space behind the barn, leading his horse. When he reached the foot of the hills he mounted and skirted their edge until he was on the south side of Destiny. Here he followed the trail taken by Pug and when he was three miles from town turned off the road and made a dry camp close enough to the trail to be awakened by hoofbeats.

He was up before dawn and moved a short distance into the hills, selecting a camping place where he could keep the trail to the south under observation. He did not offsaddle, but slipped the bit so the horse could graze and spent the daylight hours watching. Common sense told him the vigilance could not be rewarded so early, but this was his big chance and he didn't want to muff it. That night he moved to his former camping place near the road.

The next morning saw him back in the hills, impatience gnawing at him. He composed himself as best he could, telling himself that he could hardly expect the gang's return before the next evening. It all depended upon how far they had ridden and what kind of luck they had had. The day passed without incident and once more he moved close to the road.

Nothing happened during the night, although he awoke half a dozen times to sit up and listen.

He returned to the hills the next morning with the hunch that his long wait was drawing to a close. This would be the fourth day Pug and his men had been away and he could expect them back any hour. He ate sparingly and remained constantly at his watching post. Dusk fell without the gang putting in appearance and now worry began to stir within him. If they returned after dark he might find it difficult to follow Pug when he left the gang.

It was still dusk when he ventured out of the hills and took his place behind a cluster of rocks near the road. He did not dismount, sitting his saddle and smoking impatiently.

And then at last he heard the steady beat of hoofs. He pinched out his cigarette and settled into the saddle. Just enough light remained for him to see the gray ribbon of road.

The sound of hoofs became louder and he judged that the party was riding at a trail lope. He tightened the rein and waited, his face grim. They passed in a compact body, vague shapes in the dusk, and which one was Pug he could not determine.

He gave them a lead of fifty yards then spurred out onto the road behind them. He kept close but did not believe they would take the trouble to scan the back trail; they were riding easily and were evidently assured that they had shaken off all pursuit. They kept on steadily for a mile, two miles. They were less than a mile from Destiny when they halted and Brent instantly reined off the road and pulled up.

He could distinguish them as a vague cluster of men and horses, but when the cluster moved on one shadowy figure remained. A single horseman sat his saddle as motionless as an Indian sentinel, and Brent remained as silent and as still. The hoofbeats of the gang's horses diminished and were lost in the distance and then the motionless figure came alive; the horse whipped around and left the trail at an angle, moving at a slow lope.

Instantly Brent swung into the road and followed, his eyes stabbing at the shadows in order to keep the other in view. He could not hear the hoofbeats because of the sounds made by his own horse and knew that Pug would likewise be unable to hear him. The country was open for something like a half a mile, at which point a patch of pines and scrub oaks marched out from the hills to form a dark background. Against this Brent lost his quarry, but pressed onward and trusted to luck. At the edge of the trees he pulled up to listen. From directly ahead of him came the sound of breaking brush which told of Pug's passage. He urged his horse ahead at a walk, winding among the trees and dodging their limbs.

And then he heard a challenging voice, a lusty oath, and immediately thereafter the sounds of conflict. He spurred to a run, snatching out his .44.

He could see nothing and when he finally halted the sounds were close at hand and dead ahead of him. There were threshing sounds in the brush and the thud of blows and the grunts of struggling men. He dropped from his horse, let the rein dangle and ran forward. It was pitch dark here among the trees and he could see nothing but a vague shape which he knew was a horse and a rolling, twisting mass on the ground which were two men locked in combat. And even as he came rushing towards them, he saw a figure erect itself, caught the swift movement of an arm as it raised and fell, and heard the sodden thud of a gun barrel against the head of a man.

He cried, "Hold it, you!" and whipped up the Colt; and then he tripped over a root and went sprawling. He regained his feet quickly but he was too late; a figure had risen from the ground and was running towards the horse. Brent raised the Colt, lowered it again; he could not risk firing so close to Destiny. He turned and raced back to his horse, knowing as he did so that it was useless, that the other would not attempt to make contact with his boss now. When he returned to the scene of the conflict the sounds of Pug's flight had already died in the distance.

He swore feelingly. All his pains, his waiting, had been in vain. Somebody had tackled Pug and had definitely spoiled things for him. He dismounted and moved about in the brush, feeling with his feet for the prostrate body of the man who had been knocked unconscious. He kicked something yielding and thought he had found it until he stooped and touched it with his hand. It was a gunny sack, tied with a knot at its neck, and it was fairly heavy when he lifted it. He guessed that it contained the loot from the stage Pug had held up and that Pug had lost it from his saddle or had tossed it aside to provent its being taken by his attacker.

Brent glanced about him in the darkness, saw a tree with heavy branches a short distance away. He got on his horse, rode to the tree and stuffed the sack into a crotch between two limbs and pulled the foliage about it. The money had been stolen and he wanted none of it. He got off his horse and resumed his search for the man on the ground.

A groan led him to him. He stood over the fellow as he sat up and put a hand to his head. Brent stepped behind him, put his Colt against his neck and said, "Sit quiet while I look you over." He knelt and ran his hands over the man's body. The holster at his side was empty and there was no other weapon on him.

Brent asked, his gun muzzle still pressed to the other's neck. "Who are you?" The man did not answer and he asked again, "Speak up; who are you?"

The words came reluctantly. "You're that feller Tex, ain't you? Well, you might as well pull the trigger. I'm Lem Purdy."

Brent removed the gun, holstered it. He said, "You're the law, aren't you?"

"No use denyin' it now; you've caught me redhanded. But I'm warnin' you, Tex; you can kill me but they'll get you just the same. They're closin' in on Destiny fast. You and your outlaw friends are licked."

"I have no outlaw friends. You ought to know that. I came to Destiny to find the man who killed my father and my brother, and tonight you sure spoiled my chances plenty. Pug Dowd would have led me to him, and you had to pick this night to jump him. Now you'd better get back to your camp before they find you missing."

"You're turning me loose?" There was relief and wonder in the voice.

"I got no quarrel with the law. I've taken no loot and want none. Fact is, I can tell you where some is hidden right now. Come on; get moving."

Purdy got slowly to his feet. "You better make tracks yourself, Tex. And forget about the murder of your father and brother and get out of the neighborhood fast, for when the law moves in you'll be treated just like one of the others. Hell, man, you were in at least one holdup that I know of."

"That was part of the game, Purdy. I had no choice. And I'm not leaving until I do what I came here to do. Just let me sock a slug into the man I'm looking for and they can toss me into the pen."

"You're a damned fool," said Purdy shortly; then added, "but I don't know as I blame you."

He moved off a short distance and Brent heard the creak of leather as he lifted himself into the saddle. He left at a gallop, and Brent suddenly realized that he'd better be moving himself.

CHAPTER SEVENTEEN

Brent rode swiftly in a circle about the town so as to approach it from the north instead of the south. He did not don the black robe; any figure sighted by the outlaws would be fair game; after what had happened they'd hail once, then shoot. And maybe they wouldn't bother to hail once.

He briefly debated taking to the hills but killed that impulse at once. He had to be in Destiny and his best chance of getting back was right now before the alarm became general. Once on the far side of town he headed directly for the old barn, depending upon the darkness to mask his movements.

As he crossed the open space behind it, he heard the pound of hoofs in the street and the shouts of men as parties were organized. The outlaws were racing to the south, but there was the chance that they might post guards about the town, knowing that whoever had done the hijacking must be one of their own number, somebody who knew of Pug's raid and the probable time of his return.

He saw a lighted lantern hanging in the barn; it was the danger signal but he had to chance it anyhow. He rode as close as he dared then whistled a simple tune. Almost at once the light was extinguished. When he dismounted and led his horse through the rear doorway, Bub's tense whisper reached him. "That you, Tex?"

Tex whispered. "Yes. All clear?"

"I dunno. Make it snappy. They's hell to pay and somebody might come in here any minute. Gimme the hoss; I'll ride him around or they might notice he's been used. And for Pete's sake, Tex, what are you gonna do if they search the town ag'in?"

I'll think of something. I'll have to. Don't ride far; stick around and if they start searching, whistle." He unstrapped his blanket roll and mounted the ladder with it slung over his shoulder.

Once in the loft he hid the roll under some rubbish and sat down on a keg to wait the outcome of the night's adventure. Now that the excitement was over he was aware of a rush of disappointment. Of all nights Lem Purdy would have to pick this one. To recover the loot had been his objective, Brent assumed; he would not attempt any arrests until the law was ready to close in in force.

And the law was getting ready to close in. Well, it was time, but its coming might mean the defeat of his plan of vengeance. Lu had told him that the unknown leader was probably all set for a getaway. He swore in worry and exasperation. He must force the issue some way, bring the unknown out into the open, find some concrete evidence of his identity. Somewhere there must be something to betray him.

He did not know how long he had been sitting there when he suddenly realized that somebody outside the barn was whistling frantically and in an off key. He got quickly to his feet. They were searching the town! He moved softly to the window in the back and peered past the dangling shutter. A thin moon had come up and by its pale light he could see horsemen riding slowly across the open space between the barn and the hills. Guards had been posted about Destiny.

He turned away, glancing quickly about him in the darkness. He couldn't hide under rubbish; they'd find him surely and have him dead to rights. Stalls, feed bins, all would be examined. He glanced up at the broken roof. The ridge pole had broken in the middle and the ends sagged down to within five feet of the loft level, but the loft extended only a short distance and there were ten feet of open space between him and the sagging timbers. There was, however, a cross beam running from wall to wall directly beneath the broken ends and there was a foot-wide sill extending along the side wall.

Brent edged out on the sill, feeling his way with his feet and clinging to an overhead rafter until he found the cross beam. He went over it like a tightrope walker, his gaze fixed on the moonlit edge of the broken roof. He gripped the ridgepole, tested it; it sagged a bit, but held. He swung himself up, inched up the rotted boards a few feet and lay still. Beneath him in the alley he heard voices and the tread of feet. He heard men come into the stable. And Bub was still whistling.

They searched the place thoroughly, mounting to the loft with lanterns and drawn guns. Somebody said, "Any chance of his gettin' on the roof?" and another answered, "Not unless he has wings." They clattered down the ladder and went over to search Bub's shanty.

Brent stayed right there on the roof, not daring to move

until they had gone. Then he slithered to a space which was comparatively flat where he could lie without hanging on. It was well that he did so, for within an hour another party came into the stable not knowing that it had been already searched. It was close to dawn when the excitement abated and he could venture back into the loft. He did not sleep; if another search were made in the daylight there would be no escape; he'd have to sell his life as dearly as possible.

Bub did not risk paying him a visit until he fetched his supper that night. "You shore stirred up a hornets' nest," he told Brent. What happened?"

Brent told him, including his discovery that Lem Purdy was a lawman. The Cockeyed Kid had proved his loyalty and there were no secrets between them now. Bub said, "I ben expectin' it; when them last jobs of Jack's and Shotgun's went wrong I knowed they was onto us. Purdy was aimin' to git back the loot before Pug got rid of it. The whole town's plenty stirred up. Dowd said a man jumped him in the dark and dragged him outa his saddle. He had untied the sack and was holdin' it across his knees and he lost it. Said he knocked the feller out and was gonna look for it when another one jumped him and he hadda light out. He got some men and went back to look for the sack but it was gone and so was the feller he'd knocked out."

"Purdy make out all right?"

"Yeah. Biff took a bunch and rid to his camp but he was in his blankets. Biff was suspicious but they didn't have a thing on him. Most of the fellers got the hunch that the two who jumped Pug were you and the one that helped you git away that night. They figger you're doin' a little hijackin' to sorta git even for bein' run outa town."

Brent nodded grimly; it was logical assumption. But one man knew that if Brent had been one of the attackers hijacking was not his purpose, and that man would make every effort to run him down and kill him before he could accomplish that which had brought him to Destiny.

Another long period of inactivity seemed inevitable, but with the law about to close in the man he wanted would flee at the first sign of danger. Somehow Brent must get him first. Jack Roselle? Biff Williams? Cliff Durham? He still did not know.

He waited two days then said to Bub, "I'm going to search Biff's shack tonight. I want you to spot him and let me know when he appears to have settled down for the evening."

Bub did not try to dissuade him; he set out immediately for the Palace and returned within the hour. "He's at the bar at he Palace. I dunno whether he aims to stay or not, but the earlier you git on the job the better. I'll watch him and if he leaves I'll foller him. If it looks like he's headin' for the shack 'll try to git past him and whistle a warnin'."

Bub left to return to the Palace and Brent donned the shortened robe and went out into the darkness. He did not know Cliff Durham's whereabouts and must be on guard against him. He had buckled his gun belt outside of the robe and stole along in the shadows with his hands on the butt of the .44. He approached Biff's shack warily, scouting it from all sides. The black robe blended with its dark wall as he felt his way to the door and cautiously raised the latch. He entered and closed the door behind him.

He stood for a moment considering. Using a lamp was risky but he must have some kind of light for his search. He covered the window with a blanket, lighted the lamp and turned the wick low. He went to work on drawers and cupboards, looking for some writing—a note, a book of entries, anything which would give him the clue he needed.

* * *

Bub hurried back to the Palace, went inside and glanced towards the bar. Biff was not there. His crossed eyes travelled swiftly about the room. There was a man at the table with Judy but it wasn't Biff. He hurried along the aisle between bar and games searching the groups for sight of Biff. He reached the end of the layouts and saw only the bare stage before him. Biff was not in the Palace; Biff was gone.

He didn't inquire for him. He went out and started a circuit of the town, peering into every saloon he came upon, his worried gaze probing and searching. No Biff. There was only one place left—Biff's shack. He went swiftly towards it, stopping as his own shanty only long enough to snatch his gunbelt from its peg on the wall and buckle it about him.

* * *

Brent did not find the clue he sought. He found a book with notations in it, dates and amounts, and judged it to be a record of Biff's holdups. In a way it was evidence that Biff was not the man wanted because any record kept by the big boy would be a complete one of all raids. Biff was not his man.

He did find a wide floor board beneath a rag rug which came away easily when pried with his knife, and beneath the board was a hole with an iron-bound express box in it. The box was locked but Brent was sure it contained Biff's share of bank loot. He was not interested and was replacing the board when the latch clicked. He whirled about on his knees, his hand stabbing for his Colt. He did not have time to get it out; he had a hasty glimpse of an open doorway and a big man bounding towards him with curved fingers extended. Then Biff hit him.

He had no chance whatever. Biff came like a hurtling bull and he dove at Brent while he was still six feet away. He hit Brent squarely and hurled him backwards, gripping Brent's wrist as he drew his Colt. He gave a twist which a gorilla could not have withstood and the gun went spinning; then his big hands closed about Brent's throat and clamped down.

The cloth hood was of no benefit whatever; the fingers tightened like iron bands and Brent had the instant and frightening conviction that this was the end. He fought desperately, shooting short jabs at the face above him, trying to get his legs from under the great weight in order to kick. He was too close to strike effectively and Biff took the blows without even blinking.

The remorseless pressure on his windpipe did not let up in the slightest. Brent lay with his mouth open gasping for air which could not reach his lungs. The strength went out of him; his blows weakened, ceased. He flung out his arms helplessly. They were struggling near the stove and one of his hands fell and an iron poker.

A renewal of strength flowed into him. He gripped the poker tightly, raised it and brought it down hard on Biff's head. Biff winced and tried to duck. Brent struck again and again, short, hard blows. Biff cursed and let go with one hand and Brent got a fleeting gulp of reviving air. Once more he brought the poker down and this time Biff let go with the other hand and staggered to his feet. He cursed and yanked out his gun. He was standing just out of reach of Brent's feet and his fierce black eyes narrowed and glittered as he raised the Colt and pointed it at Brent's hooded head. The muzzle looked as big as the Black Hole of Calcutta.

Neither man heard the pounding boots of the Cockeyed Kid; the first intimation they had of his arrival was the boom of the gun from the doorway, and it is doubtful if Biff heard that. The bullet took him squarely in the back of the head and knocked him violently forward. He fell like a huge log on top of Brent.

The Cockeyed Kid bounded into the shack. He was no longer an old man but an outlaw with wits keyed up by danger. He snapped. "Wiggle out and let's git goin'! Come on; git up!"

Brent squirmed free and got shakily to his feet, and while

CHAPTER EIGHTEEN

BRENT knew it would not do to simply lie on the roof. The town would be like a colony of ants whose nest has been destroyed. He set about in the faint moonlight to make his hiding place more secure. There were loose boards aplenty and he arranged them across a sagging depression, laying them with calculated carelessness, and crawled into the space beneath them.

He lay there on his slanting bed and listened to the sounds which came up to him, the beat of hoofs, the calls of men to other men, the thud of boots in street and alleys. An intensive search was in progress and every outlaw in Destiny had enbarked on it.

The search was led by Cliff Durham and it was a thorough one. Private homes were roughly invaded and armed men peered into closets and attics and even under beds. Roofs were mounted and scanned, walls were examined for ropes of footholds which would enable the fugitive to descend into their depths. And constantly circling the town were horsemen with instructions to shoot anybody who failed instantly to halt when challenged.

After his encounter with Bub, Cliff had gone straight to the Palace to break the news of Biff's death and seek the aid of Jack's men. He took Jack aside and said, "It's that Tex feller; there ain't no doubt of it."

"What makes you so sure?"

"I'll tell you. Remember the night the show was in town? Well, some jigger in a black robe that covered him from hat to boots held up Sam Carter. He caught me flatfooted and batted me over the head with a gun barrel. I been lookin' for the feller ever since. I had a hunch it was Tex, but you said you'd sent him to Juniper. Now I'm askin' you, was that Tex?"

"It was," answered Jack in his toneless voice.

"Keno. Well, I was amblin' along the street when I heard the shot in Biff's shack and I seen two jiggers come out. There

k and after a while Lil went up to look for her. She
 asn't in the room. They looked all over town for her, but
she wasn't to be found. And they've been lookin' today, too."

Brent got up and paced about the loft, dismay gripping him.
He asked, "Did she take any clothes with her? Any food?"

"Nothin'. They was holdin' her clothes at the hotel but Lil
went up and paid the two dollars she owed and got 'em back.
They're all in her room. And old man Hannigan said she
wasn't in the store to buy grub and the restaurant owner
swears she didn't git any from him."

"I'm going out and look for her."

"Now you wait a minute! Set down and do some figgerin'. I
thunk of it pretty quick and you oughta, too. She wouldn't
leave town without sayin' somethin' to Lil or gittin' word to
you. When she left she expected to be right back. I'm bettin'
somebody sent her a message to meet 'em some place. Mebbe
they told her they had news of you or had fixed it so's she
could see you if she could git away without nobody follerin'
her. When she showed up, they snatched her and are holdin'
her."

"But why? And who? If Biff was alive I'd know right where
to look; but he isn't. Who'd want to hold her?"

"Reckon you can figger that one too if you take a little time.
I did; or leastwise I've got what seems to be the only answer
that fits the situation. This here big boss, whoever he is, wants
you so bad it hurts. He's scared of you, and with you on the
loose he don't know how soon you're gonna jump him and
pump him full of lead. You're too slick to git caught, and the
only chanct they got is if you git careless. How'll they make
you careless and not give a damn? By snatchin' Judy; by
drawin' you out to hunt for her jest like you said you was
goin' to do."

"Just like I'm going to do," said Brent doggedly. "If I find
the man who's holding Judy, I find the man I'm looking for.
Run up to the Palace and spot Cliff Durham for me."

Bub sighed. "I was afeared of that. You're gonna bust
things wide open and wind up a corpse. Whadda you want to
play right into his hands for?"

"Because I've got to," said Brent fiercely. "Do some more
figuring. Suppose I stay in hiding, he can't set her free now.
He'd have to get rid of her because if he didn't she'd tell who
had held her and I'd know he was my man. Damn it, we're
wasting time; get down to the Palace as quick as you can."

Bub went. Brent donned the black robe and descended the
ladder. He saddled up his horse and the mare he had bought
for Judy, for it was almost a certainty that they would have to

run for it when this thing was over. She must not remain in Destiny any longer. Regardless of his own private feud he'd take her away if he found her. *If* he found her. And if he found her *alive!*

He was waiting impatiently when Bub returned. "Cliff ain't in the Palace and I don't know where he is. Seems like they ain't nobody up there; but they's plenty fellers sneakin' around in the alleys."

"Thanks, Bub. You keep in the clear. Better go up to the Palace where you'll be in plain sight if anything happens."

"I wanta help."

"You can help better by staying out of this. If they jump me and I have to run for it I'll need you here in town to keep me posted."

Bub sighed. "All right; but I'd like it better if I was with you. I got me another gun."

Brent said, "You stay put," and went past him and into the dark alley.

He headed for Jack Roselle's house. Jack was still one of his principal suspects and with Jack and Lu both at the Palace there would be less danger getting into their house than into Cliff Durham's. He did not forget his caution; as a matter of fact he was leaning backwards to remain undetected, knowing that Judy's safety and perhaps her life depended upon his not being captured. He advanced literally a step at a time, halting, waiting, watching and listening. The slightest sound sent him to cover until he had determined its source.

He saw men, more men than one usually saw after dark. Often they were just standing in shadowy places waiting and watching. He circled Jack's house and spotted no less than three of them posted at various places. He reached the house by crawling like a slowly moving snake, erected himself under a window on the darkest side of the building and found the window slightly raised for ventilation. He lifted the sash an inch at a time until he could squirm through the opening.

Inside, he crouched, straining his ears. There was no sound. He felt his way about the room, examining with his fingers every article of furniture. There was a couch but no bound and gagged Judy was on it. When he was satisfied that she was not in that room he moved to another one.

Room by room he went through the house, downstairs and up. A light of any kind was out of the question; he had to do his searching by the sense of touch; but when he had finished he knew Judy was not in Jack's house.

He left the way he had come, studying the terrain carefully from inside before he left. He passed a guard within twenty

111

feet and might have run squarely into him had not the glow of a cigarette located the man in time.

Cliff Durham's house next.

He knew where it was, a fairly respectable log cabin at the far end of town. It was a perilous trip to make and he used the main street rather than an alley because they would not expect him to and would have posted most of their guards in the rear of buildings. He was correct in his reasoning; he saw men but they were moving from one saloon to another. The street was quite dark except for patches of light filtering from windows and these he avoided by taking the middle of the street. The thick dust muffled his footsteps.

He arrived at the cabin. It was dark and deserted-looking, and he could not spot a single watcher. This in itself was significant and the hair at the back of his neck prickled as he inched towards the door. A strange premonition of danger gripped him; this was too easy, too pat. He halted at the door and turned to peer about him in every direction. He saw nothing, heard no sound.

He faced the door again, found the latch and gripped it firmly. It was a thumb latch and it gave under pressure. Brent took a deep breath then pushed the door open. He saw nothing but a black void, but subconscious knowledge that his form would be seen against the lighter darkness outside caused him suddenly to crouch.

And as he crouched a gun blazed and a bullet tore through the black robe and the hat beneath it.

He wheeled, jumped to his left and ran. He bounded from side to side in a zig-zag course while the gun behind him thundered and lead whined past him. He heard Cliff Durham curse at each miss.

He reached the buildings on the far side of the street, and now the black robe helped for he became one of the shadows which engulfed them. But he was a moving shadow and he could see other shadows which he knew were men coming out of passageways to the street. To turn into one of these passages would be sure death; he kept to the main street.

It couldn't last much longer. Ahead of him he saw men coming at a run, a line of them stretched clear across the street. More of them were coming out of the Palace and other saloons, all with guns in their hands and murder in their hearts. He circled wide to avoid the light from Hannigan's store and as he did so three outlaws came through the doorway and one of them cried, "There he goes!" and once more lethal lead churned the air about him.

He cut across the street heading for deeper shadows; he

glanced over his shoulder and saw more men coming from the other direction. He was caught between the two groups, trapped. He came to a building with light seeping below cracks under drawn shades; its door opened and he saw a rectangle of dim light with a bulky figure showing against it. Brent had drawn his gun and he automatically lined it on the man. The man whispered quickly, "Don't shoot!" and then, "Is that you, Tex?" He was Uncle Jim Ferguson.

Tex halted, his gun still covering Ferguson. He didn't shoot because Uncle Jim had seemed to like him. His gaze flashed to the right and then to the left; the outlaws were closing in, but they had slackened their speed, sensing that they must come upon him soon, anticipating a burst of gunfire from the shadows which lay thick between the two advancing groups.

Uncle Jim whispered, "This way—quick!"

He turned and Brent leaped after him into the hallway and softly closed and bolted the door behind him. Ferguson turned left into his office and Brent followed him. The shades were drawn. Ferguson opened a heavy door and said, "In there!"

Brent entered the gloomy closet and the door closed behind him and he heard a key grate in the lock. There came a pounding on the locked front door and then the sound of Ferguson's footsteps across the floor as he went to answer it. His voice came, muffled but distinct, "What is it?"

Brent heard the sound of voices in swift conversation and Ferguson's words, "But he couldn't have come in here; the door was locked. Look if you want to."

Boots thudded on the floor as men came into the office, looked about and then went through the other rooms and out the rear doorway into the alley. From outside the house came confused sounds, the pound of boots on the plank sidewalk, the thud of hoofs in the street, men calling to one another, an occasional jittery shot as somebody fired into the shadows. Gradually these sounds diminished as the search spread to the alleys.

Brent released his drawn breath and relaxed his muscles. For the time being he was safe.

CHAPTER NINETEEN

BRENT was standing between two rows of hanging clothes, coats, jackets, woolen shirts, slickers. It was a clothes closet, narrow, five or six feet deep, as black at pitch. He moved back until he could lean against the rear wall and stepped on cloth. He bent and picked up a coat, brushed it off with his hands and hung it on a nail his fingers found.

A warm glow of gratitude had stolen over him. Good old Uncle Jim! He had been the friend in need; he had saved Brent when seemingly every chance of escape had gone. Footsteps crossed the office floor and stopped outside the closet; Ferguson's voice came to him, "All right in there?"

"All right."

"Fine! You'll have to stay there awhile. Keep very quiet."

He moved away from the door and Brent heard him go through a back room and the rear door to the alley. He returned in a few minutes and Brent heard small metallic noises followed by the clank of steel. He guessed Ferguson was opening the safe which stood in a corner of his office.

Faintly to Brent came the sound of knocking on the back door. He heard the clang of the safe, then Ferguson's footsteps as he went to answer it. When he returned there was somebody with him and when that somebody spoke Brent recognized Jack Roselle's voice.

Jack said, "No trace of him anywhere. I can't figure it out. But we know who's been helping him."

Brent felt a quick surge of alarm, fearing for the safety of Bub Whittaker.

Jack went on, "It's that Purdy fellow. He's gone. My first hunch was right; he's a lawman. And it looks like Tex is with him."

"Oh, I hardly think so. Tex helped in two of your jobs and in one of them he saved the specie. If he were a lawman he'd never have done that."

"I didn't say he was a lawman; I said he'd thrown in with

Purdy. He came to Destiny to find a man named Shell. He thinks that this Shell killed Slim Cole, and Slim Cole looked enough like him to be a cousin, maybe a brother."

There was a moment's silence, then Ferguson said in his mild voice, "I wouldn't get too stirred up about it, Jack. If Tex is after this Shell person he won't leave Destiny as long as he has a chance of finding him and with all the boys looking for him you'll round him up sooner or later."

"I'm not afraid of Tex. My name isn't Shell. What has me worried is this fellow Purdy. If he's the law he's got a pretty good line on things by this time and gone after a posse. I don't like it; I don't like it one damned bit. I'm ready to settle up and pull out of here."

"Well, perhaps you're right, Jack, but I wouldn't get panicky if I were you. Suppose Purdy has gone after a posse; he can't get to Juniper until tomorrow night and then he'll have to get men together and come back. You have a couple days leeway."

"That's not any too much time, but I'll wait and see if we lay hands on Tex Brent. By God, he can't get away every time."

They walked together to the back door and the sound of their voices faded. Brent lifted the corner of his mouth in a grim smile. Uncle Jim knew how to play the game. Brent understood now why the man was so universally liked; he could side in with you and appear to agree without really committing himself. He'd make a good executive.

Ferguson returned to the office and once more opened the safe. Brent could hear him moving about and he made several trips to the alley. This puzzled Brent until he remembered that Ferguson handled quite a lot of gold. If he were planning a buying or selling trip he'd probably load his buckboard at night when nobody could observe him. He wouldn't carry the gold openly, of course; probably had a strong box in the buckboard or, better still, a hiding place. Something like a false bottom to the buckboard. It was a good thing, he thought, that Ferguson had the good will of the outlaws. In his business it paid.

It was getting stuffy in the closet. How long had he been here? He had left the bar around eight and it had taken him at least two hours to reach Jack's house, get inside and complete his search. A good two hours. Another half hour for the trip to Cliff's cabin, moving as he had so slowly and cautiously. He had been in the closet probably an hour. Maybe more. Three and one-half hours. It must be midnight.

The air was getting foul; perhaps there was some means of

ventilating the closet. Brent took a match from his pocket, thumbed it into light and looked about him. There were no openings in the wall or ceiling, no means of ventilation of any kind and it was getting hotter by the second.

His eyes went to the coat he had picked up and hung on a nail. It was wrinkled and dusty where he had stood on it and he reached out to brush it off. Then he arrested all motion and stood staring at one of the sleeves until the match burned down to his fingers and went out. He struck another one and looked again. There could be no mistake. There was a ragged, half-inch tear in the sleeves, and the material of which the coat was made was black broadcloth.

The second match burned out and he stood there frozen, thinking fast. The man who had drugged Judy and entered her room had snagged his coat on a nail in the window frame, and the threads Brent had picked from that nail were black broadcloth threads. And this coat had been discarded, tossed to the back of the closet.

The significance of the thing reached him at once but his senses refused to credit what his mind had conceived. Uncle Jim! Surely this was a coincidence.

But was it? A train of pertinent facts started marching across his brain. Who was better fitted to lead the three outlaw bands than the genial Uncle Jim? Everybody's friend, he would never be suspected. He dealt in the purchase and sale of gold and would be familiar with the handling and shipment of specie. As a gold dealer he would be able to exchange stolen currency for miners' gold and then convert this into currency which did not bear the taint of theft. And because of his contacts and ability to move about unsuspected, he could spot jobs for the three gangs with ease and efficiency.

The sweat which dampened Brent's brow was not altogether induced by the closeness of the air in the closet. Uncle Jim! Unbelievable but undoubtedly true. Jack's visit this night, although apparently to consult a friend, confirmed it. Jack would not consult a mere friend; he was an employee passing his fears and suspicions on to his boss.

Brent reasoned it out in the closet, with outlaws thronging the streets and alleys in search of him. Ferguson was the leader of the outlaws, but was his name really Shell? Was he the man who had murdered Benjamin Hollister and Brent's brother Cole? He did not know; he would have to learn more about the man—when he had come to Destiny, where he was at the time Benjamin Hollister was murdered, whether he had had the opportunity to kill Cole. Certainly he was big enough and strong enough to transport the body of his victim to the alley where it was found.

If Ferguson were Shell, why had he saved Brent from the outlaws? Reflection brought the answer to this. Brent had surprised him there in the doorway and Brent's gun had covered him. The quick-thinking Ferguson had instantly found a way of making him secure by locking him in the closet. *Locking* him in. Brent remembered the heavy door; he was as safe here as though he were in a cell.

He moved to the front of the closet and quietly tried the knob. Yes, the door was securely locked. The door was too stout to batter down, but he could probably shoot away the lock in time. But Ferguson would never let him get away with that; he'd call in the outlaws and Brent would pay for the effort with his life. Maybe Ferguson would shoot him as he emerged in order to save that five hundred dollars reward.

And Judy! Ferguson must have her here in this house. It was Ferguson who had drugged her that night, or had Lu Roselle do it; it was Ferguson who had sent the message which had lured her to his office. He was the one man in Destiny whom she would have obeyed without question.

It was silent in the office, but even as he listened he heard slow, heavy footsteps in the hall. He remembered the staircase which climbed to the second story bedrooms; somebody was descending those stairs. The footsteps crossed the floor of the office, he heard the slight give of springs, then came Ferguson's voice, "There you are, my dear. You don't mind if I put this blanket over you, do you? I don't think we'll be disturbed but one never knows."

My dear. Judy!

There was no answer; Judy was no doubt securely bound and gagged. What was he going to do with her? Set her free after disposing of Brent or destroy her, too?

He could hear Ferguson moving about in the other room, hear the rustle of paper, the opening and closing of desk drawers. It came to him suddenly that Ferguson was preparing to flee.

And then a knocking sounded on the front door. It was a peculiar knocking, one sharp rap, then two softer ones, then another sharp one. He heard a chair scrape as Ferguson got up to answer it. He heard him walk across the floor and into the hall, heard him as he unbolted and opened the door; then came Ferguson's mild voice saying, "Ah, it's you, Jack. Come in, man; come in."

They entered the office together, Jack talking as they walked. And now his voice was not level and monotonous, it was sharp with anxiety. "Jim, we've got to get out right now. Some of the boys rode along the Juniper trail and spotted a fire. They Injuned up on it thinking it might be Tex's. There were twenty or thirty men around that fire and Purdy was one of them. I tell you they're closing in on us."

"Really?"

"You're damned tootin'. I want my cut; I'm getting out."

"Of course, Jack; of course. We'll have a settlement now."

They had halted, and evidently Jack saw Judy on the couch. He asked, "What are you going to do with her?"

"Turn her loose, I suppose. She's served her purpose; she drew Tex into the net."

"She did," said Jack bitterly, "but he slipped out again."

"Oh, no, he didn't." Ferguson sounded amused and proud. "I've got him safe enough. He's locked in that closet over there."

"Tex Brent? In that closet? How the devil did you do it?"

"He trusted me," said Ferguson simply. "Everybody trusts me. The boys were hot on his trail and I stepped outside and ran right into him. He had a gun and he was a desperate man. I brought him in—and hid him."

"Jim, are you stringing me?"

"You doubt my word? I'll prove it. Draw your gun and cover the door. . . . That's right. If he is stubborn, let him have it."

Brent heard him approach the closet and levelled with the hot impulse to fire through the door panel when he had located Ferguson's position, to kill him at whatever the cost to himself. But he couldn't do that; he couldn't risk missing and having Judy hurt for his attempt.

Ferguson's voice came from outside the door. "Listen to me, Tex. I'm going to unlock the door and you're going to come out with your hands up. Jack will be covering you and if you don't do just as I direct he'll drop you in your tracks. And it'll go rather hard with your lady friend. Hear me?"

Brent clenched his jaws. "Yes."

"Remember, your gun must be in the holster and your hands up. Ready, Jack?"

The key turned and the door opened slowly, an inch at a time. Brent peered through the crack between door and frame hoping for a sight of Jack. If he could shoot Jack before Jack sighted him, a quick leap, a whirling turn and another quick shot and that would be the end of genial Uncle Jim Ferguson. But Jack was not within range of his vision and with a fierce oath of protest Brent shoved the gun into its holster, raised his hands high and stepped out of the closet.

Jack stood close to the wall. He had buckled his gunbelt about him and the weapon which was aimed at Brent was not the Derringer he carried under his left arm but the heavy Colt with the pearl butt plates. Ferguson said, "Stand still, Tex, while I draw the fangs." Brent stood rigid as Ferguson went behind him, tugged the Colt from its holster and felt him over quickly for other weapons. Ferguson stepped away and said, "You might as well sit down."

Brent walked to a chair and sat down. Judy was lying on a couch with a blanket thrown over her. There was a gag in her mouth and the brown eyes were fixed on him in an agony of fear and desperate anxiety. He lifted the corner of his mouth in a grin and said softly, "Hello, honey. Keep your chin up."

Ferguson had moved over to the desk. He had Brent's gun in his hand. He put a hand into a desk drawer and drew out a coil of thin rope. He tossed it to Jack and said, "Tie him in the chair while I keep him covered." Jack caught the rope and tied Brent to the chair by wrists and ankles.

"Just to be sure he won't interrupt us," purred Ferguson. "Now, Jack, we'll do a little figuring. Sit down here at the desk. I'll give you the amounts and you can figure your own share."

Jack came swiftly to the desk, holstered his gun and sat down in the chair. Ferguson said, "The amounts are right there in that book before you. There's paper and pencil you can use."

Jack reached for the pencil, drew a tablet of paper towards him. He opened the record book, bent his head over it to study the entries.

Ferguson raised the gun he held and Brent saw the lust of the killer flame in his face. There was no time for him even to cry a warning. Ferguson shot Jack in the back of the head and even before the boom of the shot had died was pointing the weapon back at Brent.

CHAPTER TWENTY

JACK fell forward on the desk then toppled sideways and rolled to the floor. Brent, driven by a wild fury, strained at his bonds. He ceased his struggles when the gun was pointed at him; lust was still written on Ferguson's face and Brent knew he would shoot if all movement was not instantly suspended. But in that one brief moment of strain he had felt one of the knots about his fettered hands give slightly.

He froze, forced himself to remove his hot gaze from Ferguson and looked over at Judy. Her eyes were wide and staring and she was writhing in her bonds. When he glanced back at Ferguson the man had regained his calm; he was once more the genial, smiling Uncle Jim. He bent over and took the pearl-handled Colt from Jack's holster. "I'm afraid he won't be needing this," he said. He turned and smiled at Judy. "So sorry, my dear, but it had to be. Shotgun is gone and so is Biff; why should I share with Jack Roselle?"

"The same reasoning," said Brent tightly, "that you used with Harvey Stoat."

Ferguson smiled gently. "Harvey was a fool and all he did was leave that back door unlocked. It was I who did the work."

Brent could reach the loosened knot with the finger tips of his right hand. He set to work quietly, patiently, hiding the movements of his fingers behind an occasional twist in the chair. He said, "I reckon Cole and me had it figured about right. Stoat left the door open, you came in and hid until my father had opened the vault, then you forced him to carry the gold to the wagon you had left in the alley. Harvey sat beside my father on the seat and drove and you rode in the bed of the wagon behind them. When you were far enough from town you shot them and pushed them out of the wagon; then you drove back to the hills, unhitched the horses, lashed the gold on one and rode the other."

"Clever!" Ferguson circled the desk and sat down in a chair facing Brent. "You really guessed that?"

"My brother and I together. It had to be that way. But you made one mistake; you thought Stoat was dead but he wasn't. He lived long enough to mutter two words, *Shell* and *Destiny*. That's what brought Cole here, to find a man named Shell. And I'm guessing he found him."

Ferguson shook his head. "No, he didn't. But he would have had he lived. He did what you have not been able to do—he followed Shotgun to this house. We weren't so careful then as we are now and Shotgun was a clumsy fellow at best. No brains whatever. Cole guessed that I was the leader of the various enterprises; I'd organized the three gangs after your father's money—ah—set me up in business, shall we say?

"But Cole made a mistake; he asked Lu Roselle if she knew a man named Shell. She didn't, but she passed the question on to Jack and Jack asked me if I knew Shell. I told him I didn't, which was the truth. The name is *Snell* not Shell. Fergus Snell."

He smiled at Brent, the two guns balanced on his knees. "I invited Cole in to have a drink and a chat. I told him to sit down and went into the other room to get the liquor. I fetched a gun instead and I shot him as I passed behind his chair. He was quite heavy, but I managed."

Brent controlled himself with an effort. The knot was giving, but he must keep Ferguson talking. He said, "Did I understand you to tell Jack that you'd set Judy free?"

"Of course; but not just yet. You see, I have some things to do first. Would it entertain you if I were to tell you my plans?"

Brent told him that it would.

Ferguson was pleased. He thought quite a bit of himself and his cleverness and now he had an audience. "It's really quite simple. You heard Jack tell of the posse camped near town; they'll undoubtedly attack in the morning. They will round up a lot of outlaws, but the real prize will have flown.

"The buckboard is already loaded. The gold is in it; hidden, of course. There's quite a bit of it, you know. The excitement has died down somewhat, and anyhow everybody knows Uncle Jim. The guards will let me through without question. I'll carry Judy out and make her as comfortable as possible in the buckboard. I'm really forced to take her along for my own protection. Also I'm quite fond of her.

"When we're ready to leave I'll pour kerosene about quite liberally and when things are well soaked I'll stand in the doorway there and put a merciful bullet into your brain." He beamed happily as though he were conferring a great favor on Brent. "I'll even shoot you from the front instead of the back

121

as a mark of my respect for your undoubted courage. Then I'll flip a match into the room and—*woosh!*" He made a wide gesture with his hands.

"Lem Purdy and his posse will see the flames and come on the run. They'll be quite busy rounding up a few outlaws, and while they're engaged Judy and I will be fleeing, not towards Juniper but away from it. It's only a hundred miles or so to the border, you know. Once in Mexico, an accommodating *padre*, a short ceremony, and the distinguished *Americano* and his beautiful *señora* will proceed to scatter the gold. We may even go to Europe. Neat, eh?" He stroked his handsome beard like a peacock would preen its feathers."

The knot was giving. Brent said, "Yeah. Neat."

Ferguson got up briskly. "Well, to work." He came towards the chair and Brent ceased working, crowding his hands together so that the slack in the rope would be hidden between his wrists. Ferguson, still carrying both guns, bent over and looked at the knots which secured Brent's ankles to the legs of the chair. They appeared to be quite secure. Ferguson straightened, walked around in back and gave a casual glance at the bound hands. He said, "I imagine you'll stay put for a short while."

He thrust one of the guns into a pocket and tucked the other behind his waist band. He wrapped the blanket more closely about Judy and lifted her in his powerful arms. He looked at Brent, but Brent sat staring stonily at him. He walked into the back room, turned again to observe Brent, then went out into the alley. He was back within two minutes and he carried a can of kerosene.

He looked about him carefully, then began pouring kerosene. He soaked the couch, the carpet, the curtains at the windows; he opened the closet and poured kerosene on the clothing which hung there; he went up the stairs leaving a trail of kerosene behind him. The air reeked with the fumes; there would indeed be a *woosh* when the match was applied!

Ferguson came downstairs and into the room. He put down the empty can, glanced about him as though to assure himself that he had overlooked nothing, then walked to the door leading to the back room and turned to face Brent. Slowly the genial features hardened, the eyes narrowed and glinted, the lust of the killer came back into his face. The desk was between them but there was nothing to obstruct the bullet in its flight. He raised one of the guns.

The other hand came free!

It came to Brent then that he hadn't gained very much after all. His feet were still anchored to the chair and he had no

122

weapon. The very best he could do was to postpone his death by throwing himself forward as Ferguson fired. The second bullet would surely get him. Or the third.

He saw Ferguson's lips tighten with purpose, sensed the pressure of his finger on the trigger. He threw himself forward, diving for the desk. He heard the explosion and it seemed to rock the building. He took the chair with him, bound as it was to his ankles, and he landed sprawling against Jack Roselle's dead body. He heard Ferguson curse, wildly, viciously.

And suddenly he remembered. Jack had been wearing his belt gun and Ferguson had taken it; but there was the Derringer Jack always carried beneath his left arm! Brent's fingers dove for Jack's coat even as Ferguson started at a run to circle the desk.

The Derringer was there. He tore it from its holster, threw himself on his left side and raised the gun as Ferguson rounded the desk. He fired, first one barrel, then the other. He saw Ferguson stop as though he had run into a brick wall, saw him stiffen and then go loose like a man of straw. The hand holding the gun dropped lifelessly to his side and a muscular reaction fired the Colt. There was a roar and a burst of flame directly into the oil-soaked carpet.

Then came the *woosh!*

It was a blast that blew Ferguson back against the wall and swept over Brent like the breath from a furnace. The carpet burst into flame. Brent circled the desk, scrambling like a crab which had lost most of its legs. Somehow he reached the back room. The flames were roaring behind him.

He half crawled, half scrambled through the open back door and rolled down the steps into the cool air. On the ground he twisted about and started working at the knots which bound his ankles to the chair. His fingers were scorched and numb. He kicked out with his feet, driving the chair against the steps again and again until it fell in pieces about him. He got to his feet and staggered to the buckboard. The horses were dancing with fright.

He was vaguely aware above the roar of flames of the sound of shots and the shouts of men up the street. He calmed the horses, unfastened the traces and let them go. He ran to the back of the buckboard and looked down at where Judy must be lying. He cried, "Judy!" and got an unintelligible sound in answer. He found her and tore away the gag, then lifted her from the buckboard. Inside the house the fire was raging, spreading swiftly.

His knife had been taken so he had to work the knots loose. It took time, but presently flames burst from a window and he could see. He removed the last bond, helped Judy to her feet. She could hardly stand, let alone walk. He picked her up and ran with her into the stable. And then two men leaped upon him and seized him, and one of them said, "Take it easy, Bud."

Brent did not resist. His father and brother were avenged, Shotgun and Biff were dead and so was Jack Roselle. Judy was safe. He felt suddenly old and tired and very weak. He said, "Okay, boys," and the handcuffs snapped about his wrists.

Judy cried, "You can't do that to him! He's no outlaw!"

"We're takin' the good with the bad, sister," one of them told her. "Easy enough to sort 'em out later."

They waited until Judy could walk, then started up the alley. One of them said, "No use lettin' that fancy buckboard go up in smoke," and dragged it a short distance away from the spreading fire.

They took Brent to the livery corral and snapped one of the handcuffs to the ring in a hitching post. There were other outlaws there, prisoners, and armed guards watched them. Bonfires had been built, but judging by the glow in the sky over the Gold Exchange there would soon be no need of them.

Lem Purdy came over to where Brent stood manacled with Judy clinging to him. Lem said, "I told you to get away from here, Tex."

"I had a job to do. I did it. The man they called Uncle Jim Ferguson was the leader of the three gangs. I found it out tonight. He shot Jack Roselle rather than split the loot with him and was all fixed for a getaway after firing the town. But I managed to kill him."

Judy cried, "He's no outlaw, Mr. Purdy! You know he isn't!"

"I know he is," said Purdy coldly. "He took part in one holdup that I know of and another that I heard about. There are men here tonight who can identify him. There's nothin' I could do even if I wanted to."

"He's right, honey," Brent told her. "It's his job. All I ask, Lem, is that you look after Judy."

"I'll sure do that, Tex; I promise it."

"Thanks. By the way, you'd better get down to the Gold Exchange and guard the buckboard behind it. It's Ferguson's and it's loaded with loot. He told me there was a lot of it, well hidden."

Purdy was staring at him. He went on, "On a rafter above the first stall in the Palace barn is a cigar box with about five thousand in it, and in a tree about half a mile from town is a sack I hid filled with stagecoach loot. I found it that night you tangled with Pug Dowd. If you take me there I'll try to find the tree."

Purdy said, "Good gosh! You're tellin' me where to find a fortune you could have kept for yourself!"

Brent lifted his mouth in a bitter smile. "I told you I'm no outlaw. But some of that loot is mine; around fifteen thousand dollars that Ferguson stole when he murdered my father. If you see that I get it, turn it over to Judy to keep for me."

Purdy said, "You can gamble on that!" and wheeled and hurried away, calling a couple men to go with him.

Brent said, "You will wait for me, won't you, honey?"

She clung to him, crying softly. "Oh, Tex, does it have to be? If you tell your story, won't they let you go?"

"Maybe. I'm not counting on it. I did hold up a train—two trains; I knocked out a guard and shot another one in the wrist and got away with a box of specie. What can Purdy do?"

He held her to him and they stood there in silence, miserable, in love, the prospect of separation by gray walls for maybe ten or fifteen years looming over them. They did not notice the group of men which slowly approached, pausing before each prisoner, examining, questioning. When the group halted before them Brent looked up and knew he was doomed. Staring accusingly at him was the guard he had downed and the conductor who uncoupled the express car.

The guard said excitedly, "That's one of 'em! That's the one who beaned me and got away with that specie!"

A man wearing the star of sheriff said, "You confirm that?"

The conductor spoke firmly. "I do. I'd know him anywhere."

The sheriff said, "That settles it. Find a hoss for him and we'll take him along."

Judy sprang before Brent, her arms outflung as though to shield him. "You can't take him! I love him and you can't take him! I tell you he isn't an outlaw!" Her gaze went about frantically. She saw Purdy approaching at a run. "Ask him!" she cried. "Ask Mr. Purdy! He knows Tex isn't an outlaw!"

Purdy came up to the group, excited, panting with exertion.

"They're arresting Tex—taking him away! Mr. Purdy, please! You know he isn't an outlaw! No matter what he did, he isn't an outlaw!"

The sheriff laughed shortly. "He holds a train, bashes a guard over the head and gets away with ten thousand in gold and he isn't an outlaw!"

"That's right." It was Purdy who had spoken. "Tex is no outlaw. Tex was my undercover man."

"What!" said the sheriff. "An undercover man, and he actually kept the guards from getting back that specie?"

"That's right. He had to do it in order to find where the rest of the loot was hidden. If he'd been an outlaw he'd have killed the guard."

"And I suppose," said the sheriff, "that he located the other loot!"

"He sure did. He steered me to a buckboard that's fairly loaded with gold, and he knows where more has been hidden." He calmly got out his handcuff key and released Brent.

"Well, I'll be damned!" swore the sheriff. "Excuse me all to hell, Mr. Tex. Purdy, lead me to that gold!"

"It's in a buckboard behind the Gold Exchange. It's guarded!"

The sheriff's group moved quickly away, and Judy threw herself into Brent's arms. Then she turned and, much to Purdy's embarrassment, drew down his head and kissed him on a leathery cheek. "You're a darling!" she said.

Purdy said, "Shucks!"

The three of them walked slowly along the line of manacled, dejected outlaws. And presently they came to Bub.

Brent grinned at the old fellow and turned to Purdy. "Unlock the cuffs, Lem."

Purdy raised his eyebrows. "Why?"

"I was your undercover man; he was *mine*."

* * *

Brent Hollister, Judith Clane and Bub Whittaker rode away together. Behind them the flames still blazed, but ahead the sky was streaked with the pink and mauve of dawn. They came to a branch in the trail and halted, and Bub Whittaker said, "Wal, I'll be biddin' you youngsters goodbye and fare ye well. It shore has been a pleasure—"

Brent said, "You old catamount, you're going with us!"

A wistful hope blazed in the old fellow's eyes. "Yeah? Where to?"

"I'm getting a wad of money that belonged to my Dad. We're going to buy a ranch, a real honest-to-goodness cow ranch. And we'll need you, Bub."

"What fer? I ain't nothin' but a old throwed-away man. I ain't wuth my salt to nobody. And I won't take charity."

"Charity my eye! I tell you we need you." Inspiration struck. "We need your gun, Bub. Didn't you tell me you could draw and shoot with the best of them? We're going to new country, raw country, and we're going to find a ranch. Why, we wouldn't feel safe without you to ride herd on us! We'll even give you a title. Guardian of the J Bar B. How's that?"

A look of utter bliss settled over the old face and the crossed eyes warmed and glowed. "Guardian of the J Bar B!" Bub whispered softly, then straightened in the saddle with a new assurance and dignity. "Guardian of the J Bar B! By grab, that suits me fine!"

THE END.

MORE EXCITING WESTERNS FROM PAPERBACK LIBRARY

- ___ MONTANA RIDES! by Max Brand (52-581, 50¢)
- ___ GUN THUNDER VALLEY by Archie Joscelyn (52-590, 50¢)
- ___ GUN LAW ON THE RANGE by Burt Arthur (56-574, 45¢)
- ___ TENDERFOOT by Max Brand (52-564, 50¢)
- ___ TWO-GUN OUTLAW by Burt Arthur (56-556, 45¢)
- ___ SHOWDOWN by Max Brand (52-545, 50¢)
- ___ FLAMING GUNS by Burt Arthur (56-539, 45¢)
- ___ THE SONG OF THE WHIP by Max Brand (52-529, 50¢)
- ___ RANGE WAR AT KENO by Paul Evan Lehman (56-499, 45¢)
- ___ VENGEANCE IS A STRANGER by Jack Lewis (52-492, 50¢)
- ___ THE BORDER TRUMPET by Ernest Haycox (52-483, 50¢)
- ___ SMUGGLERS' TRAIL by Max Brand (52-478, 50¢)
- ___ CANYON PASSAGE by Ernest Haycox (52-470, 50¢)
- ___ THE RESCUE OF BROKEN ARROW by Max Brand (52-463, 50¢)
- ___ THE BORDER BANDIT by Max Brand (52-443, 50¢)
- ___ GUNMAN'S LEGACY by Max Brand (52-425, 50¢)
- ___ DEPUTY'S REVENGE by Lee Floren (56-420, 45¢)
- ___ DUEL ON THE RANGE by Burt Arthur (56-393, 45¢)
- ___ OUTLAW FURY by Burt Arthur (56-355, 45¢)
- ___ FRANK PEACE, TROUBLE SHOOTER by Ernest Haycox (52-372, 50¢)
- ___ TWO GUN VENGEANCE by Archie Joscelyn (50-343, 40¢)

If you are unable to obtain these books from your local dealer, they may be ordered directly from the publisher.

PAPERBACK LIBRARY, Inc.
Department B
315 Park Avenue South
New York, N.Y. 10010

Please send me the books I have checked. I am enclosing payment plus 10¢ per copy to cover postage and handling.

Name ....

Address ....

City .... State .... Zip ....